THE COURTESAN'S PROTECTOR

ABOUT AN EARL, BOOK 4

JESS MICHAELS

Whether the scars are on the inside or the outside (or both), this one is for you.

And for Michael, because everything worthwhile in the world is for and from you.

PROLOGUE

1805

The first time Campbell Ripley saw Jane Kendall, she scarred him.

Well, that wasn't entirely true. Robert "The Beast" MacDougal scarred him.

He'd fought MacDougal before. Several times, actually. They were billed as bitter rivals on the boxing circuits, written about in breathless terms like "vicious", "violent" and "possible to witness a death in the ring". It all brought in eyes and money and a certain fame. Ripley didn't really hate him, though. He didn't hate anyone he fought.

That didn't mean he held back on his swings, and this fight was no different. He shifted his weight as he caught MacDougal with a hard cross that rocked the other man back and cut open his lip. The sight of the blood trickling down his chin made the crowd go wild, but they each ignored that, eyes still locked on each other.

They pivoted in the middle of the ring, trying to lock back in on the correct distance for a good blow. And that was when Ripley saw *her*.

She was standing amongst the rowdy crowd in the front row just over MacDougal's shoulder, her hand tucked into the elbow of a man. She was one of the few women in attendance, but that wasn't the only reason she stood out. She was stunning, with pale blonde hair like straw and dark eyes whose color he couldn't place from this distance, but he found himself wanting to know. She had a long, slender neck and a beautiful face that a greater man might have painted, but Ripley could only gawk at.

And that was when MacDougal caught him with a hard right that threw his head back, slashed across his left eyebrow and brought a black rim around his vision that usually meant unconsciousness was about to visit. His eyebrow split open immediately and blood began to gush from the cut, streaming down his face and leaving a metallic taste in his mouth.

MacDougal gave a wide smile as Ripley lunged forward to grapple with him so he could regain a little composure. He had to get his mind back in the game, shake off the cobwebs. He shifted MacDougal with a great shove and then swung a combination of lefts and rights that sat MacDougal back and finally down where he struggled to get up and eventually waved a hand to concede.

The crowd surged forward as the promoter of the bout lifted Ripley's hand. Ripley grinned and spat out some of the blood that had gotten into his mouth, but he found himself searching the wild crowd for the lady who had so distracted him in his fight. But she was lost to the cheering, drunken masses. Gone. But as he reached up to touch the deep cut across his eyebrow that would very likely become a scar, he knew she wouldn't be forgotten.

1806

The second time Ripley met Jane, it was at a far more pleasant gathering. The Donville Masquerade, an underground club built for sin more than cards or other entertainments. It had been a year since the fight where he'd first laid eyes on her. As he'd expected, the eyebrow had healed with a bright white slash of a scar across his brow, but women always cooed over it. Men, too, if one were honest.

Here at Donville those coos usually led to a fuck. Tonight, though, as he sat at one of the tables near the back of the main room of the club, a drink in hand, he couldn't seem to muster up the interest in a fuck. At least, not with the men and women who shot him glances or bought him drinks and called him the Dragon, which was his fighting name. Not a one caught his eye.

Until *she* did. The crowd parted, almost as if the sea was being pushed aside, and there she was. The woman from the fight twelve long months before.

His breath caught as he stared at her. She was as lovely as she had been a year before. She had a different man on her arm now than she had that night. And her gown was certainly far more revealing. It was a gauzy pink so lowcut that it just barely covered her nipples. She was all fine lines and porcelain skin that he wanted to touch so badly that his palms itched.

She didn't wear a mask like so many of the ladies in attendance and he realized she was likely a lightskirt or a courtesan. He didn't care about that, of course. He lived in a world of people who made their money from their bodies, him included, so to judge anyone else who did the same would be the height of hypocrisy.

She glanced at him, almost as if she could feel the burn of his even stare, and when her gaze found his, he saw her take in a little breath. Her lips parted and she wetted them before she jerked her face back toward her companion. Ripley smiled. It seemed the lady recalled him, as well. Or at least wasn't entirely immune to him.

He pushed away his half-finished drink and stood. He'd have to be careful about this. If she was a courtesan and the man beside her was her protector, he didn't want to harm her arrangement. A woman could be ruined by a bad separation. He knew that fact far too well.

But if this was just a man paying for her company for the night…well, that was another story. He'd interrupt that without any trouble. Pay her double for her time if she needed extra incentive.

She glanced toward him again and then leaned into the man at her side, whispering to him. Her partner looked a little annoyed, but then he nodded and started off toward the back of the room where one could obtain drinks and other refreshments.

Ripley smiled and took the opportunity she had just given him. He crossed the space between them in a few long strides. She had been watching him with every step and she pushed her shoulders back a fraction when he reached her.

"I thought he'd never leave," he said softly.

The corner of her mouth quirked a little, but she blinked up at him, all innocence as if she hadn't just made this moment possible. "Oh? Do we know each other?"

He snorted out a laugh. "Ah, so it is to be pursuit. That's fine, I like pursuit." He straightened his jacket a little. "Do forgive the intrusion, miss, but I saw you across the room and couldn't bear to miss the opportunity to come meet you. Will you allow me to introduce myself, despite my very forward behavior?"

Her eyes widened a little at his suddenly polite manners. Ones that didn't fit his rough Yorkshire accent, crooked nose and scarred face. But he'd been taught well and could fit in when he needed to do so.

"Oh, I know *exactly* who you are, Mr. Campbell Ripley." She smiled a little. "Or should I call you the Dragon?"

"Ripley is fine," he said. "But you most definitely have me at a loss. I've seen you before, a very long time ago. But I never got your name—you slipped away before I could. A little like a French fairytale."

"Except Cinderella wasn't a whore." Her brow wrinkled. "Though she did make the most of a fine gown and a lost slipper."

He couldn't help but laugh, though he realized she was putting him on notice of her position in life. Just in case, he supposed, that would put him off. Intelligent.

"At any rate," she continued, lifting her gaze to his. The eyes he had been picturing for nearly twelve months snagged his and he realized they were a dark blue, like a fine sapphire. "My name is Jane Kendall."

"Miss Kendall."

"Jane," she corrected.

"Jane," he said, letting the name sit on his tongue. He motioned his head toward her companion who was now making his way back across the space toward them, drinks in hand. "And who is he?"

"*He*," she said with a sigh as she glanced at the gentleman, "is my every Wednesday night."

"Ah," he said, and looked at the man. He'd seemed to get caught up by some acquaintance he was now talking to, though he kept looking at Jane and Ripley with a thin-lipped expression. "What kind of man is he?"

She shrugged. "Temporary. As they all are in the end. But he isn't cruel and he pays well to have someone on his arm. In the end, though, I know it doesn't really matter who. He just doesn't want to go home to his wife."

"I understand," Ripley said, and glanced down at her. Their gazes met and she sucked in a little breath. Like she could see through him for a moment, see that he truly *did* understand, from a deep place he normally kept to himself.

He shook his head and reverted to playfulness to break the tension. "And what do *you* want?"

She didn't smile, but held his stare for a long moment. "For it to be worth it. The times when there isn't much pleasure. When I have to pretend it's what I desire. I want that to be worth it in the end."

His lips parted at that honesty, one he was having a hard time matching. It turned out he didn't have to. She broke the intensity of their connection as she smiled, this time with falsity, at someone just behind him.

"There you are, Gregory, you naughty boy. You took so long with the drinks."

Ripley turned and realized her lover had returned. His lips were still pursed a little as he looked Ripley up and down. "You seem to have entertained yourself just fine."

She took one of the glasses from her companion's hand and motioned toward Ripley. "I think you are a follower of pugilism, my dear. You must know Campbell Ripley. The—"

"Dragon," her companion said, annoyance fleeing. "I thought you looked familiar. I was in the crowd when you beat Tank Lewis."

Ripley inclined a head. "He was a great fighter. His recent death was a tragic loss."

Death in the ring, no less. Ripley's chest tightened. There were good ends for men like him, but there were a great deal of bad ones, too. He supposed it was the same for women like Jane.

"Oh yes, I heard he died. Seems he found a fighter that was even more of a match than you. Wish I could have been there to see it." He extended a hand. "Gregory Vaughn at your service. I'm cousin to the Duke of Bowerly."

Ripley supposed that was meant to impress him. It did the opposite and he removed his hand from the gentleman's as quickly as he could. "I think I've interrupted your evening enough. Thank you for allowing me to meet your…friend, Jane. I hope we'll bump into each other again."

She met his eyes. "I hope we shall, as well. Good night."

"Good night," he returned, and watched as she guided away the pompous arse who would have the pleasure of her company. He watched her for a very long time as she glided through the crowd. When she glanced back at him over her shoulder just once, his heart stuttered.

It was remarkable just how attracted he was to a woman he'd

seen twice in the span of twelve months. Talking to her, learning her name and the color of her eyes had only made that attraction stronger, not weaker. There was something fascinating about her. Something of strength that called to his own. It was born from pain, he knew that like he knew his own face in the mirror.

He shook his head. Lord, he was being so maudlin. That *definitely* meant he needed a fuck and to forget the pretty woman whose presence had so disrupted him not once, but twice. But even as he began to scan the room for quarry, he knew somewhere deep in his locked-up heart that it wouldn't be quite so easy to do that. Even though it should be.

~

1810

The third time Ripley had met Jane they saved a life. Well, that wasn't quite true, either. It *wasn't* the third time they'd met. They had seen each other often in the four years that passed since he learned her name. Over that time he'd watched her in hells like the Donville Masquerade as she danced by in the arms of various men unworthy of her smile, even temporarily.

She'd come to some of his fights, both with lovers and on her on. He grew accustomed to finding her in the crowd there, smiling at him as his hand was lifted. Or offering silent support when it wasn't.

She'd even attended his final fight a year before. He'd retired, taken his money and started up a boxing club for gentlemen in the heart of one of the best neighborhoods in the city. They flocked to him, begging him to teach them skills he'd taken a lifetime of pain to develop. And he took their money and had made himself richer than he ever had from any prize earned from a match, even his championships.

But even though he and Jane had danced around the edges of

each other, they'd never gotten close. He avoided her, truth be told, beyond brief conversations and those bewitching smiles. It seemed she did the same. And why not? Neither of them was a fool, after all. She very likely could see the danger getting close could create as easily as he could.

So she had become a friendly acquaintance. And if he looked for her in every hell and pub he went to? Well, that was just him passing the time.

Just as he was that night at the Painted Pony, a hell that was far more rundown than the Donville Masquerade. There were fewer rules here, too. Women weren't as protected. A fact proven when Ripley stepped outside to take a piss and there in the alley was a man, pinning a lady up against a wall. His hand was on her throat, her eye was already swelling and she was clawing at his hand, trying to push him away. From the torn state of her gown, it was evident he had already attempted or even succeeded at getting what wasn't freely offered.

There was a red anger that settled on Ripley at the sight. It was a memory as much as a reality, and one that had made him want to fight from the time he was a child.

"Oy, get off her," he barked as he started across the alleyway toward the couple.

The man hardly glanced at him. "Stay out of it, you. She owes me more than she gave and I'll take it one way or another and get me money back for my troubles."

The woman struggled, still gasping for breath as her green eyes found Ripley's in wild terror. "No, no."

"She said no," Ripley growled, and caught the man's arm to pull it away from the lightskirt.

The bastard turned and made the entirely foolish decision to take a lazy swing. Ripley caught it easily, shoved the man back and then threw his famous right hook at full strength. It hit with precision and unconsciousness was the immediate effect. The fool hit the dirty alley ground in a heap.

The woman had already started to wobble away, but she was slow in her fear and potential injury. She staggered and hit the alley wall, making little sounds of terror and pain that were likely from some far deeper place than mere physical injury.

Ripley could have left her. Or simply called her a hack and sent her somewhere else. But the look of her, tangled and dirty and trying not to sob made him think of another woman. Another life. He couldn't abandon this woman if only because he'd always wished someone would come to the rescue of the other.

"Miss," he murmured, approaching her.

"No," she whispered, and raised her hands, swatting at him.

"I'm not going to hurt you," he promised, and reached for her.

To his surprise she darted out a fist and caught him on the jaw. The punch wasn't perfect or practiced, but it had heat behind it. His jaw stung and that was something.

Her eyes went wide and she lifted her hands to cover her face, as if she feared he'd hit her back. Not the worst assumption considering what she'd already been through. Instead, he caught one of her hands and lowered it.

"I'm not going to hurt you," he repeated, as calmly and firmly as he could. "But you're in no state to get home. Let me help you. I've a rig just up the way. Where can I take you?"

She looked him up and down, uncertain and trying to determine his character with little clues. She glanced back toward the man in the alleyway. He was starting to stir now. Swear a little. She shivered.

"I'll go with you," she whispered. "But I don't want you to—"

"I won't," he said. "My promise won't mean anything until I keep it. Come on."

He had a phaeton, which he only ever took to places like the one he was at now when he might need a way to escort someone back to his home above his club. Tonight he was glad to have it for a far different purpose. When they reached it, the lady allowed him to help her up and she settled herself as far away from where he would sit as she could.

"I'm Campbell Ripley," he said as he grabbed the reins and knickered at the horses to move. She relaxed a little when he needed both hands to drive the vehicle.

"I know that name."

"I was a fighter," he explained.

She nodded. "Yes. A—a champion."

"I was," he said. "But now I'm just a man who'll need to know how to get you someplace safe. Will you tell me where you live?" She hesitated and he turned his attention fully to road ahead so she wouldn't feel ogled. "Or the home of a friend if you prefer me not to know where you stay."

She was silent for a long moment and then gave him an address. He didn't speak as he drove her along, and though he still felt her tension and her fear and her pain, she seemed a little more comfortable.

As they neared the place she had told him, she glanced at him. "My name is..." she hesitated again. "Esme. I'm Esme."

"Esme," he repeated gently, and looked at her from the corner of his eye. "How badly are you hurt?"

She touched her face. The eye the bastard had punched would bruise. He had the impression that had never happened to this woman before. Perhaps she was new to the game. Though she certainly knew how to throw a punch by nature, at least.

"I can't answer that question," she said on a shaky breath. She waved toward a small building. "That's the one."

He pulled the rig to a halt and got down. She was already trying to climb down herself, but as she did so she lost her balance and slipped. He caught her with both hands and supported her as she tried to recover herself. Before she could, the door to the home where they'd stopped flew open and a woman raced down.

"Esme?" she called out.

Ripley jerked his head up and stared, for he knew that voice. Jane came to a halt and stared right back.

"Ripley?" she said, blinking in shock.

"Jane?" he said in return.

Jane shook her head and once again her attention turned to her friend. "Oh, Esme," she burst out, and rushed forward to grab Esme's other arm.

Esme collapsed against her a little, the tears beginning to fall and her breath coming shorter. Jane glanced at Ripley over her head. "Help me get her in, will you?"

He nodded and together they entered the small home. Once inside, Jane nodded toward a parlor off the entryway. "Wait there, if you will. The hallway is too narrow for all three of us to pass like this."

He released Esme and watched as Jane shored her up and took her down the hallway, whispering soothing nothings to her as she went. He drew in a long breath and then entered the parlor Jane had referred to. At last, he felt like he could look around and so he did.

The place was small, but there was a touch to it that made it feel like home. There were two worn chairs before the fire and Ripley took one to wait and then got back up when he realized he'd sat down on some needlepoint. He pulled the piece from under himself and looked at it. It was a very pretty piece, a bouquet of flowers, and nearly finished. Was it Jane's? He had a hard time picturing her as a handiwork person. But then again, most women were taught such things and he had no idea of her past. Of her life beyond those brief glimpses at hells and fights where both of them were playing the role others expected.

He set the piece aside on top of a book set on the small table between the chairs. He tilted his head and looked at the title. It was a gothic romance that was all the rage at present. He had never been a great reader, though he could read. His mother had insisted on that.

"Ripley?"

He pushed to his feet and faced Jane as she entered the room. "Is she badly hurt? I didn't want to push her too much."

"She's bruised and battered," Jane said with a frown pulling down her lips. "But I think it's the heart hurt that stings the most. She cried herself out pretty quickly after telling me most of what happened."

He nodded. "I think I might have been too late for the worst of it."

"No, you saved her from the very worst. Dead is worse," Jane said, and shivered as she crossed to a painted sideboard across the room. She poured herself a whisky and did the same for him. When she brought the drink to him, he saw her hand was shaking.

She sat in the chair beside the one he had vacated and he returned to his own. They sipped their drinks in silence for a few moments.

"What's her story?" he asked at last.

Jane glanced at him and for a moment he thought he saw a flash of something in her eyes. It was gone before he could identify it, though. "The same as most of us, I suppose. She ran from something at home. I found her on the street, ready to get herself into worse trouble without even knowing it. I couldn't save her from everything, though." She looked at the door.

"I don't think it's your place to save her from everything," he suggested.

She sighed. "I suppose not. She doesn't come from our life, though. Our kind of past."

He nodded. They'd never discussed their pasts, but he'd always guessed they had a similar one. Poverty and pain often recognized each other.

"She does this work," Jane continued. "She is good at it. I mean, you look at her pretty face and of course men want her."

Ripley blinked. He hadn't really given much thought to how Esme looked, beyond her injuries. He supposed she was pretty, now that he considered her. But nothing compared to Jane.

"How long has she been doing this?"

"Months." Jane sighed. "She hates it most of the time, I think. But how else can women like us make it?"

Ripley found himself touching his jaw. It was a little tender from where Esme had punched him earlier in the night. "She cracked me after I took care of the bastard who did that to her."

Jane's eyes went wide. "Did she?" She smiled. "Good girl."

He laughed a little. "It was a hard punch."

"That's a compliment coming from *the Dragon.*"

He shrugged. "I'm not opposed to compliments. Given or received. I wonder if she might want to learn to throw that punch with more purpose."

"From you?"

"Yes." He took another sip of his drink. "I run a boxing club now, for toffs with nothing better to do than spend their money pretending to be rough. Well, some of them aren't so bad. But I also train fighters who actually compete. Including a few women."

She drew in a long breath. "Esme as a fighter?"

"I don't know," he said. "One punch landed well doesn't mean much. But at the least she would have more options in her arsenal for the next poxy fuck who tries to hurt her."

Jane's lips tightened. "And at the most?"

"Perhaps she'd find a different way to support herself if she hates doing it from her back so much," he said softly. "Making money from your body can come in many forms."

"And the life isn't for everyone," Jane agreed with a sigh. "Let me give her a few days and I'll...I'll talk to her about it. Bring her by your place to let her see for herself if she wants to try."

"Do you need the address?" he asked.

She stood and he did the same. "No, Ripley. I already knew about the club. I think it's wonderful you've been able to find a different way out. Through. You should be proud of yourself."

He felt a ripple of that pride work through him at her words. As if her offering him that allowed him to accept it instead of brush it off because it felt too sharp and breakable. They stared at each other a long moment and then he smoothed his jacket.

"I-I should leave you to your friend," he said. "And I look forward to hearing from you—er, her—er, you both, soon."

She smiled and motioned him to the door. There they both paused and she stared up at him, those dark blue eyes focused entirely on his face. Her stare froze him there, unbreathing, as if that would disturb the moment.

"Thank you for saving her," Jane said softly. Her hand came up, her fingers stroked over the roughness of his cheek. And just as he'd always known when he pictured her touching him over the years since he'd first seen her, it was heaven. It was heat. It was everything.

But she pulled away and broke the stare before it could move to anything else. "Good night."

He nodded. "Good night."

And then he left her, his hands shaking, his heart beating hard in his chest. He drove away and everything that had told him he had to be very careful about this woman screamed even louder now after he'd felt her touch.

If Esme agreed to his suggestion that she learn to fight, he and Jane would be closer than ever. He'd have to figure out how to maintain distance if he wanted to survive that unscathed.

CHAPTER 1

1812

Jane Kendall stood in the middle of the shop and looked around, wondering at the fact that it was *hers*. After a lifetime of roughness and pain, a life she'd accepted and even enjoyed from time to time, this new venture still felt...odd.

It was her friend Esme's fault. Though Jane supposed she couldn't call her Esme anymore. She was now the Countess of Delacourt, after marrying her earl just a few months before. Esme was back in Society where she belonged. Jane was happy for her.

But she also felt such...loss. Of her friend, of her regular life. She never said it, of course. Esme and Delacourt had so kindly helped her, she didn't want to be ungrateful. And yet she was...*bored* by being settled. Bored and out of place.

The bell on the shop door rang as it opened and she jerked herself back into place and time. She forced a smile to her face, one that fell as the woman who had entered on a gentleman's arm glanced at her. She knew the lady. Intimately. It was the Viscountess Bowerton and the gentleman with her was her husband.

She swallowed and stepped forward. "Welcome, my lord, my lady."

The woman halted in her steps and stared at her a moment before she turned up her nose without acknowledging Jane and walked away to look at a few items on a display closest to the door.

"Good afternoon," the gentleman said, oblivious to the tension between the women. He looked around. "You must be Miss Kendall. I think you took over the place from Old Weasley a few months ago, yes?"

She nodded and glanced at the viscountess again. "Er, yes. I assume you were a patron of his. I hope I shall provide the same service that he did."

From across the room, the viscountess snorted. Her husband looked at her, his lips pursing, and then nodded and went to the other side of the room to browse alone.

Jane's heart was pounding. She hadn't run the shop for long and though she had considered the fact that a former lover might, in fact likely *would*, one day come through her doors, it was quite another thing to actually experience it. And to have it be Elizabeth Bowerton, a fine lover but not a particularly nice person even when they'd occasionally met for sex years before...well, that made it all the more uncomfortable.

She fiddled with some items in a display case in front of her, half-watching the viscountess as she huffed around the store. At last, she glanced over her shoulder at her husband and then stomped over to Jane. She glared at her and in a harsh whisper said, "I didn't know it was *you* who took over from Weasley."

"Yes, my lady," Jane said softly. "I'm sorry it's a surprise to you. But I-I assure you I would never say anything about our...previous arrangement."

The viscountess's eyes narrowed and she leaned over the counter so that her pretty face was just before Jane's. "That sounds like a threat. A reminder that you could use what you know against me?"

The bell at the door rang again, but Jane didn't look. Instead, she sucked in a breath. "N-no, not at all. I was truly only trying to put your mind at ease that—"

"You must be aware that I could far more easily destroy you than you could ever hurt me," the viscountess continued as if Jane had said nothing. "Do you think *anyone* would shop here if they knew that a former whore ran the place? That she might have opened her legs for their husbands...or occasionally their wives? You'd be shunned, given the cut direct."

"I think that's enough."

Jane jolted at the interruption from behind the viscountess. Both women turned toward it at the same time and heat filled Jane's cheeks as she realized it was Ripley who stood there, his handsome face impassive even if there was tension to every muscle in his body.

The viscountess glared at him. "And just who the hell are you to tell me such a thing?" Ripley tilted his head and said nothing, just stared at her, unspeaking and unmoving until she shifted. "Another one of the whore's lovers? Of course."

She pivoted and stomped across the room, raising her voice as she said, "Come along, Bowerton, I think the quality of this shop has gone down significantly. I cannot imagine shopping here anymore."

The viscount looked confused at the sudden and very rude order, but he followed his wife out like a whipped dog, the ring of the bell echoing in Jane's ears as the door slammed behind them.

She rested her hands on the countertop and took a few breaths before she lifted her eyes back to Ripley. She had always been fascinated by his face. It almost surprised her every time she saw him and marveled at the chiseled angles of his jawline, the dark focus of his eyes. Christ, even that slash of a scar across his eyebrow gave him a rakish look. His tall, broad-shouldered beauty was a bit of a balm on her soul, even if she wished he hadn't been involved in this humiliation.

"That seemed personal," he said softly.

She shrugged. "An old lover."

His brows lifted. "And the wife was confronting you over it?"

"*She* was the lover," she said with a laugh. She had no concerns at Ripley's reaction to that revelation. Some might be shocked at the idea, but she knew his proclivities. They seemed to be of a mind that pleasure was pleasure and the source was not that important.

He nodded. "Ah, I see. And was the lady always so... disagreeable?"

"Never quite so directly cruel, no," Jane said. "And her fire was much more endearing when it came with money to soothe it. I think it was a shock to her to see me here, twisted further into her world than I ever was before. I'm sure her husband doesn't know she takes female lovers. I'm *certain* she never told him she's never orgasmed with anyone but a woman." She sighed. "She has to strike before I do and I don't doubt Elizabeth will."

"You think she'd try to ruin you?" Ripley asked.

"She said she would. Right before she called me a whore and you so kindly interrupted like a knight to the rescue."

Ripley's mouth tightened. "Not a knight, I assure you. Just a concerned friend."

Jane stared at him a moment. Over the past few years, they *had* become friends. After the training he'd offered on that horrible night years ago, Esme had become a fighter in his stable. She had bloomed, even before she found the love of her life and married, returning to the world where she belonged. During that time Jane had struggled being so near the man before her, but she'd found ways to do it. To cherish what he was and not hope for what he could have been if it was a different world or a different life.

But there were times, like now, when he stood close to her and she could see the fascinating bend of his nose up close, the arch of that scar across his eyebrow, the fullness of his lips and she longed to fall into him.

Only once she started falling for a man like this, there wouldn't be an end to it. She would fall forever and that was terrifying.

"I'm happy to have such a friend," she said with false brightness. "But you cannot have come here today only to save me from demons draped in diamonds. Were you here to shop my wares or for some other reason?"

He smiled a little, though it didn't reach his eyes. "Actually, I've come on an errand from mutual friends. Delacourt was at the boxing club this morning and he brought a personal invitation to a fete he and Esme are hosting next week. He mentioned you hadn't responded yet and asked if I would check in with you."

Jane bent her head. "Oh. Yes, the invitation. I received it a few days ago."

"But you haven't answered," he said evenly.

"No." She sighed. "It isn't that I don't want to see Esme. I miss her terribly. But…"

"But she's back in her world."

Jane nodded. "And if that encounter you interrupted tells me anything, it's a stark reminder that I don't belong anywhere near that world. I hardly belong in the one where I currently reside."

Her hands were still clenched on the countertop and Ripley reached out to cover one. He never wore gloves and so it was his bare skin that touched hers. She sucked in a breath as she lifted her gaze to his. There were only a few times where this man had ever touched her over the years and those fleeting grazes always stirred such things in her. Heated desires and dangerous hints of emotion.

"Esme loves you," he said.

Jane struggled to find her breath and her words. To break the spell of this moment somehow. At last she turned to frivolous flirtation, always a refuge with this man. She slipped her hand away from his and said, "I know. Everyone does."

He smiled a little at her playful response. "How could they not? Truly, Jane, do come. I'll need saving from the fops at the very least."

She arched a brow. "You? The Dragon needs saving from a bunch of ladies and gentlemen in frilly costume?"

"The Dragon isn't allowed to respond like he would in the ring," Ripley replied with a laugh.

She sighed again and then nodded. "For you and for her, I'll be there. I'll send word to them today."

"Good." He inclined his head slightly. "And now I must get back to my club before Brentwood allows them to have full brawls in the middle of the main ring."

She smiled at the mention of Ripley's right-hand man. He was a serious sort, so the idea that he'd let those who trained there do anything wrong was laughable. "Oh yes, wouldn't want that to happen. Good day, Ripley."

He moved to the door and gave her a little bow. "See you soon, Janie."

Her heart fluttered at the endearment he sometimes used. Fluttered even more as she watched him walk out her door, down the street through the shop windows with that casual grace that flowed through his big body. And though she would see him again in just a few scant days, she still felt the little ache that always tightened her heart whenever he walked away from her.

The one that she feared would bring her to her knees in the end, no matter how carefully she avoided that outcome.

Brentwood was conducting lessons with a group of gentlemen when Ripley returned to the club. From his hard expression as Ripley came through the main chamber, his friend was irritated.

"Keep the hands up and continue," Brentwood said as he ducked under the rope of the ring and started toward Ripley. "You're late."

Ripley laughed. "Sometimes it's unclear to me who is the boss in this scenario."

"No, it's not," Brentwood said, and there was the faintest hint of humor in his dark eyes. "But you should know that the Marquess of Honington is waiting and he isn't amused at your tardiness."

Ripley rolled his eyes. "I'd say he could take it out on me in the ring, but the man has been taking private lessons for over a year and has yet to perfect a right that does anything beyond a tickle."

"I might not open your conversation with the gentleman that way," Brentwood said. Ripley shrugged from his jacket and began to loosen the knot of his cravat. Brentwood watched him for a moment through narrowed gaze. "You're dressed rather nicely. Where did you go exactly?"

"Checking up on me, eh, Mother?" Ripley said, and pulled the long length of the cravat free. He placed both on the back of a chair and stripped off his shirt.

As he tossed it on the pile, Brentwood said, "Were you off with Jane, then?"

Ripley glared at him before he took a seat and began to unfasten and remove his boots. "I was asked to take care of something that had to do with her, so yes."

"She hasn't come around as much since the Hellion retired."

Ripley flinched. Hellion had been Esme's fighting name. "No, I suppose she hasn't."

"But you can't stay away."

Ripley rolled his eyes. "I swear, a man makes one little drunken statement about a completely understandable attraction and his friend can't let it go."

"Because it isn't about one drunken statement," Brentwood said. "And you know it."

Ripley let out a long breath. "What do you want me to say? Jane is living her life, I'm living mine. We both keep a distance beyond what can barely be classified as a friendship. That's the end of it."

"I'll remind you of that next time you're in your cups spouting bad poetry about the beauty of her hair."

"Fuck off, Brentwood," Ripley said with a chuckle that belied the sting that statement left in its wake.

Brentwood shrugged and returned to his group and Ripley tried to pull himself together as he approached the red-faced marquess who awaited him in the smaller ring in the back of the room. The man looked truly irritated to be kept waiting, so perhaps he'd actually swing when they sparred today.

And if Ripley knew anything, it was that the feel of taking a punch could sometimes ease the ache of a broken heart. He looked forward to it.

CHAPTER 2

When Ripley accepted Delacourt's invitation to a fete at his estate, he'd expected it to be a large gathering where he could fade into the woodwork except when someone from the club recognized him. Or an old admirer from his boxing days. He had ready responses for that and in the end, those who approached him weren't really interested in *him*, just what they believed him to be.

But he was surprised to discover, as he was led to the parlor where he had been told the rest of the party was gathered, that it was an intimate group.

Delacourt crossed to him after he'd been announced, hand outstretched in what seemed to be genuine friendship. It was returned, in truth. Ripley liked Delacourt. He was good for Esme and good to her, which was even more important. And he had a wicked right cross that anyone could respect.

"Ripley," he said as they shook. "I'm so glad you made it."

Esme was already coming across the room toward him. Ripley smiled. She was no longer the terrified woman he'd saved in an alleyway. Nor was she the rough fighter he'd helped her become. She was lovely in a green gown that matched her eyes. She looked like a lady.

And yet she still grasped his hands with both her own. "Campbell," she said with a smile. She was one of the few people who ever referred to him by his first name.

"Es," he returned, and lifted her hand to his lips for a brief kiss. "You look well."

"I'm more than well," Esme assured him. "You know some in the room, I think. Ramsbury goes to the club with Finn, I know."

"Ripley," Ramsbury said. "And you've met Marianne."

"My lady," Ripley said to Ramsbury's wife. She was a lovely woman, quiet but always kind. And from the way Ramsbury sometimes went on about her, deeply loved.

"And these are our very good friends, the Earl and Countess of Kirkwood."

Ripley nodded at Kirkwood, who also belonged to his club, though he didn't attend quite as often as Ramsbury and Delacourt. "My lord. And it's a pleasure to meet your wife. I've heard a great deal about you, my lady, all good things."

The countess, a pretty petite woman with dark hair and eyes, smiled broadly at him. "And I of you, Mr. Ripley. All these gentlemen have such high regard for you, it's impossible not to admire you without even knowing you."

"Ah," he said with a smile. "I'll try not to let you down with the reality."

The group laughed at the quip and Ripley realized in that moment that Jane wasn't there. He wrinkled his brow. "But where is Jane? Miss Kendall, I mean?"

Esme's lips tightened a fraction. "Not here yet. Though she did say she was coming, so I still have hopes she'll do so."

"Perhaps she just wished to be fashionably late," Ripley suggested, but he doubted that was true.

As the group fell back into conversation that he tried to follow while he watched the door, he worried the inside of his lip. Jane wouldn't want the attention that fashionably late would bring, especially if she had, just as he had, believed this was a large fete.

He shifted his weight a little as discomfort rose in him. She wouldn't just not show up without sending word. Had something happened? He couldn't help but be dragged back to a few months before when Esme and Delacourt's troubles had led to an attack on Jane. The fear from that night returned far too easily and he was so focused on it that he jumped when Delacourt touched his arm.

"Worried?"

"Me? Never," Ripley lied. "She did say she would attend."

Delacourt held his stare a moment and then nodded. "I'm sure she will."

Just as he said it, the butler appeared in the door again and said, "Miss Jane Kendall, my lords and ladies."

He stepped away and Jane entered the room. Ripley couldn't breathe for a moment. He'd seen Jane in all kinds of dress over the years. Seductive as a courtesan, barely covered so that there was little imagination to her shape. But also comfortable and casual in the home she once shared with Esme. And of course, he sometimes saw her dressed for her duties as shop owner, where she was staid but fashionable to send a message to those who entered her place.

But he had only ever seen her dressed as formally she was now once before. At Esme and Delacourt's wedding ball she had worn the same gown that draped across her body presently. A dark blue with a crisscross pattern on the hem, bodice and at the end of the short, puffed sleeves. Her hair was done up simply, but she didn't need frivolities in order to make her beautiful. Her long neck, her pale skin, her dark eyes, her full lips. Everything about her was stunning and he was, as ever, stunned.

"Jane!" Esme called out, and hustled across the room to throw her arms around her friend.

Jane squeezed her back and then looked around the room. "Oh, am I early?"

"Late," Esme teased. "It's only us friends tonight."

Jane glanced at Ripley for a moment and he saw her swallow

hard. Like him, she didn't feel comfortable in such a small group of very important people. It was harder to hide.

He gave her a smile that he hoped would shore her up and she returned it a little weakly, but she allowed Esme to take her arm and all but drag her into the group. She was introduced and re-introduced to all in attendance and Ripley was pleased to see how easily she was accepted by Lady Ramsbury and Lady Kirkwood. Both were kind women and if they knew what Jane had once been, they didn't seem bothered by it or by her current standing in life, despite it being so different from their own.

Still, he could feel her discomfort, see it in the subtle shifts of her body, the tightness of her smile, the way her fingers occasionally clenched around her drink. After a little while, she stepped away from the circle of their friends and glanced toward him. Her shoulders relaxed a fraction as she crossed to him at the window.

"Were we tricked tonight, do you think?" she asked without any preamble.

He laughed. "You also thought it was going to a ball or some other big, ridiculous fete?"

She nodded. "And yet it's just a few friends. No hiding for us outcasts." She caught her breath and looked up at him. "Obviously you aren't—"

"Of course I am, Jane," he said and looked toward the three earls across the room. "I like them. They're the best one can hope for in men of their rank. I would call Ramsbury and Delacourt at least passing friends. But I am definitely an outcast."

"Well," she said, and lifted her glass as if to toast him. "Then I say to the outcasts. May we survive the well-meaning intentions of our rich, bored friends."

"I'll drink to that." They both laughed as they did so. Before they'd finished drinking, the butler reappeared.

"Supper is served," he intoned.

The couples began to pair off and line up to go to the dining room with much laughter about what rank went first. Jane and

Ripley hung back together, watching it all, that feeling of being an outcast even heavier.

But at last the pairs began to walk to the dining room and Ripley offered an arm to Jane. "May I?"

She hesitated a moment and then slid her hand through the crook of his elbow. That touch, just like the touch earlier in the week at her shop set off fireworks of electric desire in his body. But he was good at controlling his body, so he knew he didn't show it.

They made it to the dining room and he escorted her to the chair in front of her nameplate. As he slid out her chair, she looked up at him with a warm, gentle smile and once again his heart thudded. At her, at this. At everything he would deny to everyone else around them but couldn't deny to himself.

He stepped away and went to his own seat to settle in for supper. But as he smoothed his jacket and smiled at Ramsbury, who was seated next to him and had asked him some question, he glanced once more at Jane.

This woman was the love of his life. But that gave him no joy, for he knew it would never be spoken. To do so was to open himself up to too much potential for pain. He wouldn't allow it. And he knew she wouldn't either.

If asked, Jane would have said that it had been a lovely gathering. It wouldn't be a lie. Despite her knowledge that she didn't belong in the hallowed halls of earls and countesses, these particular ones were nothing but kind. They treated her as an equal and it was easy to like Marianne and Clarissa, which was what they demanded she call them, just as she adored Esme.

And yet she'd been on edge all night. On some level, that was simply how she lived her life. There had been too many years of danger to lose the habit of preparing for the worst. But it was more than that, too. Having Ripley in the room was comforting, but it was also difficult. To look over and watch him talking, smiling, laughing. To see him watching her and feel heat suffuse her cheeks like she was some innocent maiden rather than a jaded former lightskirt who already knew that depending on a man, even one who was good, was the path to destruction.

Campbell Ripley was a mistake she couldn't make. And yet reminding herself of that fact got harder every year, with every little interaction where she felt the weight of his regard press down on her and tempt her.

"Oh, Jane, your hair really is so pretty."

Jane blinked and looked over to find the Countess of Kirkwood, Clarissa, had been the one to speak. "Thank you," she said with a smile as she reached up to touch her simple chignon.

"I've always envied beautiful women like you or Esme with your bright locks."

Marianne, the Countess of Ramsbury nodded. "Oh, I have too. I always thought my plain brown was so boring."

Esme laughed. "Your dark hair is gorgeous, both of you!"

"It is," Jane agreed. "That diamond clip in yours, Lady Ramsbury...Marianne, is especially lovely. It really draws the eye."

Marianne touched it and blushed. "Sebastian gave it to me a few days ago. He spoils me."

Jane smiled. Marianne looked so truly happy that for a moment her chest hurt. It had been easy to tell herself love didn't really exist after all she'd seen and done. After all the men who were betraying their wives and families by burying themselves in her body, and other pleasures they kept away from those they claimed to protect. But being around these three and their husbands all night had been a reminder that for some that golden glow of true connection did exist.

She bent her head focused on her madeira as the others chatted about their husbands for a moment.

"You and Mr. Ripley have been friends for a long time, haven't you?" Now it was Lady Kirkwood who questioned her and once again Jane jerked her attention back to her companions.

She glanced at Esme with a laugh, happy to have a distraction from the meat of the statement. "*Mr. Ripley*. When you called him that, did he flinch?"

Esme laughed along with her, for they both knew the man well after so many years. "It's hard to fathom referring to Campbell with such formality."

Jane's lips tightened. Esme was the only one who ever called Ripley by his first name. That fact had occasionally made her a little jealous over the years, even though she knew perfectly well that her friend considered him more like a brother.

"He's very interesting," Marianne said. "I understand from Esme and from Sebastian that he's led a fascinating life."

Jane thought of the years she'd known him, about his powerful career as a pugilist, about how he'd pulled himself from that life and created a whole new one, a very successful one, with his club. "Yes. Fascinating."

Esme arched a brow. "I think my two dear friends are trying to pry very politely into what the two of you are to each other."

Jane swallowed. "What we are?"

Marianne and Clarissa exchanged a look. "He's very handsome," Clarissa said carefully. "And he always seems to be watching you. You are very comfortable when you're talking. It does make one wonder if there might be something more, something deeper than the friendship we understand you two share."

Jane looked at Esme. "You aren't involving yourself in this silliness, are you? You know that Ripley and I are friends. There's nothing more to it."

"Isn't there?" Esme asked, and there was no teasing to her tone.

"I think I'll get more madeira if I'm to entertain such foolishness," Jane said with a forced laugh as she walked away to the sideboard.

When she was no longer facing the other women, her smile fell. Her heart was racing. She knew none of them meant any harm. All of them, her dear friend included, were just rich, bored women, just as she'd told Ripley. They'd found love and they wanted to see it everywhere else they looked. It was kindly meant, but they didn't understand her world. Even Esme, who had inhabited it for several years, had only been a passing visitor. They didn't understand that love was a liability for some. That it could create weakness. Cause pain.

"Why isn't this whisky?" she muttered as she picked up the bottle of wine and began to uncork it.

"I have whisky."

Jane jumped as Esme appeared at her shoulder like a wisp. She laughed as she bent to the cabinet at Jane's knees and brought out a bottle. She waggled it playfully and then poured it into Jane's empty glass.

"Are you well?" she asked as she did so.

Jane gripped the glass tighter. Once upon a time she might have poured out her troubles to her friend. But that was when she was just Esme, champion female pugilist and runaway heiress.

But now she was Lady Delacourt. Charlotte Esmerelda. A former lightskirt couldn't give over her troubles to someone with all those honorifics, could she?

"Of course," Jane said instead.

"The shop is going well?" Esme pressed.

Jane swallowed. "Yes."

She hoped she didn't sound as uncertain as she felt. It wasn't just that the visitors to her general store were few and far between, probably fewer and further between since Elizabeth had made her unpleasant stop there a few days before. It was that when Jane was in the shop she felt…itchy. Uncomfortable. Out of place.

Esme had meant well in helping her procure the place, helping her step away from a life made on the wages of sin. But it didn't feel like a place that…fit.

"I'm worried about you," Esme said, taking her hand and squeezing. "Worried about us. I don't see you anymore and I miss my friend."

Jane shut her eyes and hated that tears stung behind them. Ones she refused to allow to fall. "Oh, you know how it is. Just so busy. And you are, too. A freshly married lady must have all kinds of things to do. Both the mundane and the much more exciting if the way Delacourt always has to touch you is any indication."

Esme's expression softened. "He is wonderful. I do adore him to distraction. But I'm never too busy for you. If you need me, I'll always be here."

Jane was mercifully saved from having to answer that statement by the gentlemen returning to the room together after their port and billiards. Esme squeezed her hand and returned to Delacourt, as the others did to their own husbands. But Ripley didn't come to her as he had earlier in the night. He smiled at her, but then he went to the fireplace and lit a cigar.

And she was left alone. Which was what she'd always claimed she wanted: to be independent. And yet it didn't feel as good as she wished it was.

In that moment, it felt empty.

CHAPTER 3

A few days had passed since the gathering at Esme and Delacourt's, but Jane still found herself out of sorts. She kept thinking of the conversation started by countesses. The one that questioned what her relationship with Ripley was, exactly. Put that together with the emptiness she felt sitting for hours in her lonely shop and…well, her head was not a good place to hide at present.

She sighed as she began the process of shutting the shop down for the night. There had only been one customer today, an elderly gentleman who had spent time pursuing her general goods but had ultimately only bought a few sweets. She reorganized shelves that hadn't even been touched, dusted off countertops and eventually moved to the door to pull the shades and lock up.

Before she could, the door opened and a young man stepped in.

"I'm closing up, but if you're looking for something in particular, I can help you," she said, forcing a smile to her face.

"Oh no, miss, I'm not a customer," he said. "You've a message."

He held out a letter and when she took it, he bobbed away. She frowned as she locked the door behind him and then went to the candle at the counter so she could see better. She had no idea who might write her. Messages from Esme always came from her servants, who had a recognizable livery. Friends from the life often couldn't read or write. She, herself, had been taught to read by Esme only a few years before. The handwriting of the address wasn't from Ripley.

With everyone she could imagine might write to her eliminated, she found dread creeping through her. Finally, she broke the wax seal and unfolded the page. There wasn't much to it.

Miss Kendall,

I'm sorry to tell you that your sister, Miss Honora, has disappeared from the grounds of our fine seminary. We have put forth a search before this writing, but she seems to have vanished entirely. In the weeks leading up to the disappearance, several of her schoolmates and instructors noticed a change in her behavior. A sense of distraction and a generally disruptive attitude. And, as you know from other notices, Honora has often thwarted authority and was already on her final warning.

We leave this matter in your hands now with our best wishes.

Miss Gwendoline Knightly

Headmistress, the Knightly Seminary for Young Women

Jane crumpled the letter against the counter, her heart beginning to race. It was panic that rose up on her. Terror that clawed at her and nearly brought her to her knees right there in the middle of her hated shop. All she could think about was Honora and her bright eyes, her loud laughter. Honora as a little girl, the last time she'd seen her sister.

And now she was gone. Missing, perhaps run away. But perhaps something more sinister. She stared at the letter again and then rushed to the door she had just locked. She fled into the street, hastily hailing a hack and directing it where to go before she flung herself inside, letter still clutched in her shaking hand.

She only had one person she wished to see in this horrible moment. Only one person she needed to see like she needed her next breath. And if he couldn't help her, then she feared no one could.

~

It had been a long day at the boxing club. Wednesdays were always his busiest and saw many a man come in and out of the doors, either for group practice or personal training. At the end of the day, Ripley actually enjoyed the ritual of cleaning the ring up, putting the practice equipment away. It was mindless, repetitive, a way to quiet his normally busy mind, if only briefly.

So he stood in the middle of the center ring, still shirtless after his last training session, washing away the collected sweat of earlier fights from the ring floor. He could hear Brentwood shuffling around him, organizing things.

"I can do the rest," Ripley said. "Go on home. I'm sure Mariah must be waiting."

Brentwood gave a little smile at the mention of his wife, inclined his head and took in a breath to reply, but before he could there was a racket of pounding at the locked door. They exchanged a quick look and Brentwood shrugged. "If I'm about to leave, I can answer and send anyone away who doesn't have legitimate business."

"Thank you," Ripley said, and went back to his mopping. There was something about the wild pounding, though, that distracted him from the duty. He stopped his work, leaned on the handle of the mop and watched as Brentwood unlocked the massive double door.

When he did, Jane stumbled inside, half-collapsing in a heap on the floor before his right-hand man.

"Miss Kendall!" Brentwood exclaimed, catching her arm.

Ripley was already moving. He bounded over the top ropes and rushed to her, dropping to his knees when he reached her and gathering her closer to hold her up.

"She's gone," she gasped out.

He shook his head even though terror filled him. "Who? Who is gone? Esme? Was she taken?"

"No," she said.

He was relieved at that. Esme had been in danger not so many months ago. That danger had also reached Jane and she had been kidnapped, hurt. Sometimes he had nightmares of that horrible day. Of seeing her tied to a chair, so small when she was normally so confident and certain and unflappable.

"Then who?" he asked gently.

"My—my sister," she stammered.

A sister? Ripley hadn't even known she had one. A secret she kept close to the chest, protected from strangers and even friends. He looked up at Brentwood, who appeared nearly as concerned as Ripley felt. She didn't need an audience for whatever was about to come. He shook his head and then said, "I have her, mate. I'll call for you if I need anything."

Brentwood hesitated but then nodded. "Yes, Ripley. Good night."

He left then. When he was gone, when Ripley and Jane were alone, she leaned forward and rested her forehead against his bare chest and she began to cry softly. His heart felt like it was being torn in two. He'd never seen Jane cry before. She was too tough from a life of hard edges and difficult choices. But now the sound of her pain and grief was like an injured animal howling around him.

He gathered her up, tucking her against him, and carried her across the hall and up the narrow stairs toward his personal chambers above the club. She hiccupped into his neck as he did so, the soft stir of her breath against his bare skin a distraction only metered by her pain.

He carried her to the small parlor just inside the entryway and placed her on the settee, then set a fire to warm the room and lit a few lamps. She had stopped crying by then and when he faced her, she was watching him.

He poured her a whisky, handed it over and took a place beside her. He was suddenly aware of how small the settee was. How close he had to sit to her.

"Breathe," he said gently. "And drink that."

She nodded, sipping the drink and taking a few shaky breaths. Then she looked at him again. "Please help me, Ripley."

He nodded. He couldn't have denied her anyway, but certainly not with her in this fragile, vulnerable state that he doubted she'd shown to anyone, even Esme, in years. He took her hand and lifted it to his chest.

"I will. But first you must tell me everything."

Everything. Jane shivered at the idea. Had she ever told anyone in her life *everything*? There had been half-truths. Just enough to explain. Little lies to soften. But the whole truth was something she kept locked in her heart, tucked away where it wouldn't hurt her or anyone else.

And now Campbell Ripley held her stare and asked for everything. And she wanted to give it. To offer her secrets because she knew he would protect them. Guard them. Even to his own detriment.

She thought of Nora and nodded. "I'll—I'll try," she whispered. "I have a younger sister. Eight years younger, eighteen just a few weeks ago. Her name is Honora...Nora."

He said nothing but just kept holding her hands, massaging gently.

She continued, "She's been at a school for girls for half her life. I sent her there."

"Why?" he asked.

She squeezed her eyes shut as images of anger and pain and drunkenness bombarded her. All those things she'd tried to protect Nora from.

"Our mother," she said. "She's…difficult. Unkind. Like me."

His brow wrinkled and he leaned closer. "You are not difficult and you are so kind under that tough exterior you show the world."

She stared into his eyes and could almost believe him. After all, Ripley didn't lie, did he? She broke the stare because it drew her in too easily.

"I meant she was…is…a lightskirt." She stood and paced away from him, needing distance from his intensity when she told the story. "She didn't know who my father was. Just another customer. And she never tried to protect me from her work. She'd bring in men past me, close the door and I'd sit in the parlor and cover my ears."

She heard him make a small sound, but didn't dare look at him over her shoulder. It was better to keep staring out onto the street. Count the carriages as they passed by in the inky night so that she didn't get lost. Get emotional again. That was weakness.

"When I was seven, she met a blacksmith and somehow convinced him to marry her when she became with child. Nora was born two days after my own birthday. We became a family, but not a happy one."

"He wasn't kind."

She did look at him then and held his eyes evenly. "No. Not to me, not to my mother. Eventually, not to Nora. None of us mourned when he died in a fire. But he left us with nothing and it didn't take three months for my mother to return to her old ways. I was fifteen by then. I watched her drink herself into oblivion and drag man after man through our door. And I had to protect Nora from that. From her…and…and from me. I started the trade at fifteen myself—I had no other choice, we needed the money. But I didn't want my sister to follow that path. So I sent her away to protect her from that life. From my mother, from me."

He winced. "So she's been at school ever since."

She nodded. "But this afternoon I received this." Her breath hitched as he took the missive. He unfolded it and read the blunt words from the headmistress.

"I see."

"She ran away." Jane bent her head. "Or disappeared. Oh God, maybe she was even taken? All I can think of are all the possibilities. Whatever it is, it's not good. I wanted so much more for her, Ripley. More than this. More than *me*."

He crossed to her then in a few long steps. He shook his head and fire flashed in his dark eyes. "Stop saying that, Jane. Stop acting as if you and your past are why this is happening. You did for her what many wouldn't have. You offered her a better life than the one that was foisted onto you. You are her hero, not her villain."

"She wouldn't agree," Jane said, and now the tears filled her eyes again. "She despises me. She thinks I've kept her from our mother, from whatever fairytale life she imagines she would have lived back at home. She stopped answering my letters two years ago. I *am* her villain."

He took her hands and pulled her closer, just as he had when she collapsed on his doorstep. But this time she wasn't quite as overwrought and she realized she was pressed to his bare chest. A very muscular, very warm chest.

"You are perfect, Jane," he whispered.

She hesitated and then she lifted her chin, leaning up toward him in what felt like half-time. She knew when he realized what she was doing by the way his body went rigid with awareness and his breath got shorter. She should have pulled away, but she couldn't.

Not now when she felt so weak and needed his strength to keep her steady.

"Jane," he said softly. A warning, a reminder.

"I don't care," she whispered in answer.

He let out a ragged sigh and then his fingers slid into her hair, holding her steady before his mouth found hers.

The kiss was featherlight at first, gentle, soothing. She gripped his bare forearms, palms tickled by the light smattering of hair there, and found herself falling into him the way she'd always feared.

And when he deepened the kiss? When his tongue came out to trace the crease of her lips and urged her to open to him fully? She dove, not fell. She wrapped her arms around his neck, let out a needy sound that echoed in the stillness around them, and met his tongue with her own.

Desperation was what followed. Heated, passionate, long-with-held desire that had always hung between them but never been acted upon. And now the dam broke, pressure too much, and she dug her nails into his shoulders. He moaned in response, such a lovely vibration that rolled through her body and made her ache. Oh, how she ached for him. For this. For everything.

She wanted *everything* and that recognition sank in beyond the pleasure of his touch and the desire that sparked between them. She couldn't want everything. That was far too dangerous.

Slowly she pulled away. He let her, though they stayed in each other's arms, staring at each other in the flickering lamplight. At last she set a palm on his chest and pushed back, freeing herself from his embrace.

"I'm sorry," she whispered.

He didn't say anything about that apology. He simply let out a long sigh and shoved a hand through his hair, mussing the dark, thick locks. "I'm going to help you, Jane. I'll help you find her."

She swallowed. "How?"

"Let me put on a shirt and we'll figure it out," he said as he walked past her out of the parlor.

She turned back to the window and set her palms against the cool glass. She wanted the shock of the temperature to give her purchase, but it didn't. Ripley had kissed her and it opened a floodgate she feared she wasn't strong enough to close. One that would end in heartache.

She already had enough of that thinking about Nora and wondering where she would sleep tonight. Was she afraid? Alone? Or with someone who would hurt her?

"Oh God," she whispered.

All those things were why she needed to stop focusing on Ripley and get her mind where it belonged: Nora. There was no future in anything else.

CHAPTER 4

Ripley stood at his armoire, shirt crumpled in his fist, trying to calm the racing of his heart. He hadn't intended to kiss Jane when he made his argument against her belief that she was somehow the cause of her sister's current problems. But then she'd looked up at him, dark blue eyes rimmed with more tears, cheeks flushed with emotion and need. All he'd wanted to do was hold her. Like she was his.

But she wasn't. Jane didn't belong to anyone. She made certain of it. Her independence was a shield. A wall. He wasn't certain he was strong enough to climb it. He'd tried once, years ago by asking her if she ever considered finding someone to be with permanently. To love. Her quick dismissal of that notion while she held his gaze let him know she wouldn't entertain any overtures. He'd respected that and never brought it up again, sticking to their friendship even though it ached.

But she needed help. She needed a friend rather than just another man who panted over her and took advantage. He needed to be that friend.

He slung the shirt over his head, buttoned it and rolled the sleeves. With each movement, he took a deep breath, refocused on what *she* needed not what he wanted when her warmth seeped into him like the sun cutting through winter clouds.

When he returned to the parlor, she was still at the window, but she was no longer looking out onto the street. She held the letter in her hand and was reading it over and over.

He crossed to her and slipped it away gently. She looked up at him and his heart stuttered yet again, but this time he maintained control.

"Come, you need to eat," he said.

She blinked. "Eat?"

He laughed at the utter confusion on her face. "Yes. Food. It's called supper."

To his relief, she smiled at the quip. "Oh, is that what fancy gentlemen call it?" she asked, even as she followed him down the hallway, into the kitchen at the back of building.

He motioned to a rough wooden chair at the small table in the room and she took it, watching as he gathered what he'd planned to eat for the night. He had stew leftover from the previous evening and he put the pot on the fire to warm as he cut a few slabs of bread from a loaf and hunks of cheese to join it.

"I don't think you'll find it fancy now," he said with a little smile as he poured her a glass of red wine to join the meal.

"It smells divine, though," she said. "I'm more shocked to see you cooking. I never pictured it."

"How do you think I eat?" he asked with a chuckle. "Or what?"

"Fire and brimstone," she said.

"Oh, because I'm the Dragon?" He ladled stew into a bowl and set it before her, along with a spoon and a napkin. He set the plate with bread and cheese, along with salted butter, between them and then joined her at the table.

"I always thought the Dragon fit you," she said as she buttered her bread. "Powerful. Sleek. Dangerous." She hesitated and then lifted her gaze to him. "Beautiful."

He swallowed his sip of wine, feeling it stick in his suddenly thick throat. "Beautiful?"

She shrugged. "You know that you are."

He didn't know that. To him beautiful meant soft and gentle. He wasn't those things. He'd forgotten how to be over the years where he made his money through violence. He still did, actually, just training others to take and throw the blows. How was that beautiful?

"Eat," he said, and motioned to the stew cooling in her bowl.

She did so and for a short time there was only quiet between them. He could feel her unwinding from the terror of finding out her sister was missing. Her shoulders relaxed, her expression softened. That was what he wanted, but he hated that he had to break that now. That he had to drag her back to her fear.

"If your sister ran away…" he said at last, and just as he thought she would, Jane tensed. "Where do you think she might have gone?"

Her lips tightened and she set her napkin on the table beside her empty bowl, shoving both away. "The last time she wrote to me," she said slowly, the pain obvious in every word, "she told me that I couldn't keep her from our mother forever. That one day she'd go to her and there was nothing I could do about it."

"You think she might have made good on that threat after all these years?" Ripley asked softly.

She let out a shuddering sigh. "It would be the best of a horrible group of options. Which is saying something."

"Then we should start there," Ripley said, and stood to clear the table. When he faced her, he leaned against the edge of the basin table and folded his arms. This was for her good, not his own. If he continued to sit too close to her he was going to touch her again. To offer comfort and he didn't want to violate her space. "Where does she live?"

"Little Oak," she said, and her voice wavered.

His brow wrinkled. "I'm not familiar."

"It's a pleasure village just outside of London. A little like Bath, though not quite as fine. It's half a day's travel."

He nodded. "Then we'll go tomorrow."

"We?" she repeated with a shake of her head as if she didn't understand.

"I told you, I'm here to help."

She leapt to her feet and took a few steps toward him, nearly closing the distance that separated them. "But your business, Ripley!"

"You have a business, too," he pointed out.

Her brow wrinkled as if she couldn't recall what he meant. "Oh, the shop. Oh God, the shop. Well, I'll simply close it. It's hardly successful at any rate."

He stared at her a moment. Esme and Delacourt had gifted her the shop recently, so perhaps Jane was still adjusting to the way it worked. But he sensed it was more than that. Often she seemed… disconnected when he visited her there.

"I can't ask you to do the same," Jane continued.

He shrugged. "I'm not closing the club. Brentwood will take care of the management. It will make no difference at all. Even if it did, I'd still do it."

"It would be…good to have you there," she said softly.

That admission, even said so softly and in such a shaky tone, meant the world to him. He did take her hands then, reveling in the weight of them in his own. "Janie," he said, reverting to the pet name he sometimes used for her. "We'll find Nora. I promise."

There was a deep sadness in her eyes in response. Both of them were too savvy, too aware of the unfairness and cruelty of the world, to believe that statement. It was a promise he might not be able to keep, something said to soothe her in this moment of high terror.

"I know you'll try," she said at last. She stared up at him a long moment and her fingers flexed against his. Her thumb stroked across the top of his hand and he shivered. Then she bent her head.

"I-I should go home. I should prepare for the trip and whatever we might find there."

He nodded. That was best, even though he wanted so desperately for her to stay. To offer himself in a way that would only complicate things even though it would be unforgettable.

"I understand. Let me take you."

She looked like she would argue, but then her shoulders rolled forward in surrender. "It would be nice not to try to find a hack."

He led her back through the narrow hall, feeling her presence at his back the entire time. Offering to help her was the right thing to do, he had no doubt about that. He wouldn't, couldn't, leave Jane to suffer alone.

But he also had no doubt that by the time this was over, the ache in his heart would be far deeper, because time spent alone with her couldn't help but change him. It always did.

Ripley's phaeton wasn't a new one, but it was well maintained. It was one of his few frivolities, something Jane had always been fascinated by since the bouncy, jaunty vehicle seemed at odds with the serious, focused man who now drove it through the streets back to her shop and the little home she kept above it.

Still, the cool night air on her face was helpful at present. It kept the pure terror over her sister at bay, settled her. As did the presence of the man beside her. As if he sensed that, his hand came over to settle on her knee gently.

The weight of his fingers was powerful, soothing and erotic at the same time. Her hand trembled as she covered his, splaying her fingers so that they fit into the crooks of his bigger hand. For a few moments they rode silently like that, the weight of everything hanging between them. But also the relief of his presence wrapping around her like a cloak.

After a short ride, they arrived back at her shop. She stared at the sign that swung from the awning as they stopped. This was home, but it hadn't yet begun to feel like it. She feared it never would.

She looked at Ripley and squeezed his hand before she released it. "I don't deserve you."

His expression softened in the dim light of the street lanterns. "Oh, Janie, you deserve so much more," he whispered. He cupped her cheek, rough fingers brushing her skin. She found herself leaning in to him, felt him do the same even when her eyes fluttered shut.

He kissed her again. Only this time the heat didn't elevate, the passion didn't threaten to bubble out of control. This time it was only comfort.

When they parted, he said, "I'll pick you up here tomorrow morning. Is seven too early?"

She shook her head. "I'm learning to be an early riser. And for my sister? I'd do anything."

He helped her down and sat while she unlocked her door. She looked back at him before she entered the building, her knight in an open carriage. Then she shut the door to him.

But she worried that having him help her with her sister was likely going to keep her from being able to shut the door to him ever again. That she would open herself up to emotions she'd tried to avoid, desires that had long simmered and a heartbreak she might never recover from. And pain along with it. The kind she knew she could cause him, just as she'd done to so many others.

Finding Nora, though, it would have to be worth it.

CHAPTER 5

There had been no sleep the night before. Jane had tried, of course, knowing she needed to be sharp the next day. Her adversary always was, after all. But thoughts of Nora plagued her. When she did briefly doze off, her dreams had been even worse. Her younger sister fighting off the same demons that had eventually claimed Jane, herself. Or worse.

Still, she didn't feel tired as she stood at her window, watching down at the street below for Ripley and his phaeton to collect her. She'd had thoughts of him, too. Of his immediate offer of help and of his kiss that had brought both peace and even more confusion to her restless body.

She was surprised when a carriage stopped on the street before her shop. A customer? It was far too early for that, though she supposed they would see the sign she'd made and hung on the window, declaring the shop would be closed for the day.

But it wasn't some stranger who stepped from the rig—it was Ripley. Even from a distance, she knew him. She had for years, knew the way his body moved, knew the way he held himself both in combat and at ease. And when he looked up toward her window, her heart skipped in a way it most definitely shouldn't.

She turned away and hustled down, locking up after herself as she stepped up to him.

"Good morning, Jane," he said softly as he reached out a hand to her. She took it and let him help her into the rig. He joined her, slipping into the seat across from her, his long legs edging into her space a fraction. Then he knocked on the carriage wall and they began to move.

"What is this?" she asked. "I thought you only had the phaeton."

He smiled a fraction. "Keeping track of me, are you?"

She returned the smile and searched for the teasing pepper that had always led their relationship. She needed to get herself back together at least when it came to him. "You need a minder, I think."

"You might not be wrong about that," he said softly. "But the carriage isn't mine. Brentwood has one. He married last year and his wife, Mariah, brought a little money and a carriage and driver to the settlement. Apparently her parents couldn't imagine life without a rig."

Jane pursed her lips. "Must be nice."

"Isn't it just? At any rate, he was kind enough to loan it to me, as I didn't think you'd want to rumble along for half a day in the phaeton and I wasn't certain I could find you a horse quickly enough."

"Oh," she said, and thought of Ripley's always-frowning right-hand man. He was very good at his job, anyone who interacted with him for more than a few minutes could see that. And he was fiercely loyal to Ripley. Which made the way he sometimes glowered at Jane feel even more pointed.

"Well, I suppose he doesn't need one more reason to dislike me," she said with a sigh.

Ripley tilted his head. "He doesn't like you?"

She lifted her brows in surprise. "I'm shocked you weren't already aware. You always notice the little shifts and moods of everyone."

"A survival technique in my former business."

She smiled weakly. "And mine."

"Is he rude to you?" Ripley continued to press, and she saw a flicker of anger enter his stare at the thought. Gone immediately, but heated for the flash it had existed.

"Oh no!" she said. "Never rude. Just...cool. I felt he was pleased when Esme stopped fighting and that meant I came to the club less often to corner and support her."

Ripley seemed to consider that. "Hmm. Well, I'm sorry you feel that way. Brentwood is serious, that is very true. Sometimes he's hard to read, even for me. I suppose that's part of why he's so good at his job. His reactions are inscrutable most of the time and when things get heated at the club, you need a man who doesn't add to the upset."

"I can see that. Certainly I wasn't saying it to impugn the man. I know he's vital around the club and a good friend to you."

"He is that," Ripley mused softly. "If he doesn't like you, he's never told me. And if he had, I wouldn't give a damn."

"No?" she said, truly surprised at that answer, despite the tension that had always existed between her and the man across from her. She'd been in the world long enough to know that one friend could poison the other against someone he was attracted to. Men tended to stick together, an often-terrifying united front since they held so much more power.

"No," he repeated. "Because *I* like you."

That sentence was said lightly, perhaps to lift the heavy mood in the dim carriage. She'd known it, of course. Ripley liked her. Ripley wanted her. But Jane still felt a thrill at it. Far more deeply than she ought to considering the circumstances.

"Flatterer," she said with a laugh that swiftly turned to a sigh. She rested her head back on the seat cushion and thought of what he would see today, the kind of welcome they would likely have. "I know I've dragged you into a mess. Perhaps you won't like me so much when this is done."

He held her stare evenly for what felt like an eternity, though it couldn't have even been thirty seconds before he spoke. "Do you know who my mother was?"

She blinked at what felt like a change of subject. "No."

His mouth tightened, as did his fists on his thick thighs. "Regina Ripley."

Her mouth dropped open and she leaned forward. "The—the famous courtesan?"

He nodded slowly. "The very one. Famous, celebrated and, sadly, far too long dead. I couldn't judge you, Jane, because you and I are cut from the same sad and tattered cloth."

Ripley very rarely spoke of his mother. He'd stopped a decade ago when the cancer had taken her. Even those he'd call friend didn't know his relationship to her, though people remembered her. She had been the belle of her time, the most sought-after courtesan in all of London.

"I've seen Bernard Horner's portraits of her," she said. "So I know she was stunning. But what was she like?"

"Horner," he repeated with a shake of his head. "One of her old protectors. She was his muse. I was an extra nuisance around. Regardless of all that, it's nice to see her face when I encounter the portraits in galleries."

He didn't mention the one in his residence above the club. Jane hadn't gone into that particular parlor where it hung above his fireplace.

"It must be startling," Jane said softly. "Painful, even, if you were close."

"We were," he said. "You asked what she was like and she was kind and lively...but she was also sad. When she stripped away all the trappings of her sophisticated life, she was wounded."

Jane's nostrils flared slightly and he wondered if she was thinking of her own life as a lightskirt and mistress. She hadn't often reached the lofty heights his mother had, almost always keeping herself to middle class men and women. But she understood. He sometimes saw that same wound in her.

"Was it just the life that hurt her?" she asked gently. "Or something more specific."

"Yes, the life was hard. You know it. Not always bad, but difficult. But I think what truly broke her was my father. Lord Pottinger."

"The earl?" Jane gasped.

"I thought you didn't know an earl from a marquess?" he said with a laugh that felt forced. It was forced.

"Esme's gossip sheets forced the toffs on me. And the earl is in them regularly. He's your father?"

Ripley nodded, trying to keep the sour taste in his mouth from becoming an equally sour expression. "The very one. He used her until she had nothing left to give. Until his son swelled in her belly and then he abandoned her with not even a farthing of support. We don't talk. He can get fucked."

She met his stare and he knew she saw past his façade. She measured his pain. He supposed that was what they'd always done to each other. The only two capable of such an action. That was part of why they constantly pulled away from each other. And part of why he loved her. To be seen was…something. Even if it scarred. He touched his eyebrow briefly out of habit and then cleared his throat.

"We struggled most of my life. She was celebrated, but the men who bragged about having her in their bed weren't exactly generous. I started fighting at seventeen to help out. Was rubbish at it at first."

"Did she ever see you come into your own?" Jane asked.

"No." He said it and that one syllable burned like fire. "She died a year and a half before I went on the jag that led to me taking the title. She never fully benefitted from my success."

He dropped his gaze from hers. Jane could see many things, but somehow he didn't want to share his guilt. That he hadn't had enough to get his mother better doctors. Or at least allow her end to be more comfortable. That was the ultimate regret of his regretful life.

Jane was quiet a moment and then she motioned to the book he had placed on the carriage seat before he came to pick her up. "What are you reading?"

She was allowing him respite from the painful subject. He appreciated it and picked up the tome. "*Gulliver's Travels*," he said. "An adventure to pass the time if you'd like. We could read it out to each other."

Her cheeks flamed briefly. "Oh...I only learned a few years ago." She turned her face as she said it.

He wrinkled his brow. He hadn't known that. Of course it was very common for those of their class to not read. His mother had taught him from the start, telling him it would give him an advantage. She hadn't been wrong.

"Well, I could read it to you if you'd like," he said.

She nodded. "Yes. I could use the distraction." She settled back and closed her eyes.

He watched her for a moment, memorizing her face when she wasn't observing him in return. Then he pulled the curtain away from the carriage window to give himself more light and opened the book from the beginning, a note from the publisher to the reader.

"*The author of these Travels, Mr. Lemuel Gulliver, is my ancient and intimate friend; there is likewise some relation between us on the mother's side.*"

Despite the desperate nature of their travels out to Little Oak, there were times on the trip that had actually felt *comfortable*. Where Jane could almost forget her fears for Nora, her anticipation for what would happen when they saw her mother, and what stirred when Ripley was so close to her.

He'd read her the adventure story, giving it life, and she had been allowed to lose herself a little. And when he stopped? They'd talked. Not about his mother or her family, but just about life. About the friends they shared.

But now the carriage slowed as they reached their destination and Jane's comfort was long gone. She reached across the carriage and caught Ripley's hand in both of hers, seeking reassurance.

"She's…" she began. "I don't know what to expect, Ripley, and I—"

He leaned forward and cupped her cheeks. He kissed her once, gently and far too briefly but it quieted her mind for a blissful moment. "I'm here."

He released her and opened the carriage door, stepping out first before he helped her down. She knew she was digging her fingers into his bicep as they faced the old house together.

It was the same as it had ever been, and yet somehow worse. Her mother hadn't kept it up over the years and the painted shutters were peeling, the front garden overgrown so that one had to trod on the weeds to get to the front door.

The very door that was opening now and revealed her mother. There was a moment where the two women stared at each other and a lifetime of memories overwhelmed Jane, left her unable to speak.

Her mother seemed to have none of that problem. She looked her daughter up and down, folded her arms and said, "Well, look what the cat dragged in."

CHAPTER 6

The woman before him was drunk. That was obvious by the slur in her harsh words. But if the way Jane shrank a little at his side was any indication, the cruelty to her mother's expression wasn't something new. Jane's hand gripped even tighter on his bicep and he reached over to cover it, but she didn't look up at him.

"Mama," she said softly.

"Well, come in." her mother said, turning her back on them dismissively. "There'd be no way to keep you out, I'm sure."

They entered the ramshackle home and followed the woman's weaving steps through a shabby hall and into a parlor. It was filthy and packed with things: trinkets and broken furniture, a discarded glove draped across the back of a chair, dirty slippers perched dangerously close to the fire.

"Mama, may I present Mr. Campbell Ripley," Jane said, her voice trembling a little.

Her mother pivoted back and looked him up and down. "I know that name," she hissed, eyes narrowing. "Ripley...Ripley..."

Ripley stepped forward. "Perhaps from my days as a fighter, Mrs. Kendall."

"Yes, the boxer," she barked out. "And I'm not Kendall. That's *her*. My dearly departed husband's name was Winchester."

He inclined his head. "My apologies, Mrs. Winchester."

But she was already glaring at Jane again. "Well, at least you've got good taste in your lovers. Does he support you well? Enough that you could spare more money at last?"

Jane's jaw twitched and her cheeks actually flared with color. "Mama, that's enough," she said softly, calmly.

Ripley knew that tone. The one a person used when trying to calm an often-riled beast. He'd heard it from himself many a time when he didn't want to fight a drunken man who wished to prove himself by taking a swing at a former champion.

To have to use it for one's own parent? His heart ached for Jane.

"Why don't you sit?" Jane continued. "I could get you tea. Does Roberts still work for you?"

Her mother flopped into a chair, grabbed for a half-empty drink beside her and snorted. "Roberts left years ago. A woman from the village brings food a couple times a month. She always pesters me to pay her to tidy up, but what can I do when you give so little? Are you offering more?"

Jane's lips thinned. "I'll see if I can find...find help for you, Mama." She drew in a shaky breath and for the first time she looked at Ripley. He saw her pain. All that deep pain she was so careful to hide. The display of it felt like a knife to the gut. He held her stare a moment and then gently nodded, encouraging her.

"Mama, I came to talk to you about Nora. She's missing."

Ripley forced himself to look at Mrs. Winchester, to read her just in case Jane was too wrapped up in her own reactions to see little tells that might help their cause. But to his surprise, her face was entirely blank.

"Who?" she asked.

Jane's mouth dropped open. "Nora, Mama." Still no recognition dawned. Jane's voice lifted, anger and hysteria barely contained "*Honora*. Your youngest daughter."

"Oh, *Nora*." There was the recognition, but still no emotion to go with it. She glanced at Ripley. "Did Jane tell you about her? She stole her, you know. So be careful. If she ever provides you with a bastard, she'll be certain to take that one, too. Probably use him to bleed you dry."

Ripley winced at her cruelty. Not only toward Jane, but at her utter disregard for her missing daughter. She was more interested in hurting her eldest to give a damn about her youngest. Mrs. Winchester drew in a breath as if to continue her screed, but Ripley stood.

"Madam, that is *enough*," he said, keeping his tone soft but firm. That was for Jane's sake, not hers.

He glanced down at Jane, wishing he could pour his strength into her. Wishing he could carry her off and make all this disappear. Now that he understood it, he wanted to save her from all of it.

"*Where is Honora?*" Jane asked, carefully emphasizing each word that came out through clenched teeth.

Mrs. Winchester finished her drink before she said, "I don't know."

"Please, this is important. More important than any hatred you've developed toward me over the years," Jane said. "Did she come here? Did she contact you?"

Her mother smirked. "I thought you forbade it."

Jane's eyes came shut and her tone was sharper. "Please!"

There was a moment's pause and Mrs. Winchester rose, crossed to the sideboard and grabbed for a bottle there. She poured more amber liquid into her glass. "I haven't seen or heard from her. But you're overreacting, I'm sure. She's what? Twenty now?"

"Eighteen," Jane said softly. "Only just."

"Then she can do as she pleases. She'll show up."

Ripley's stomach turned. This appalling lack of care for either of her daughters made Jane's reasons for denying her access to Nora very clear. But he also believed that this woman hadn't seen or heard from her youngest. He didn't think she'd be able to keep herself from crowing to Jane if she had.

"What about money, Jane?" her mother pressed.

Jane rose a little unsteadily and smoothed her skirts. "I'll arrange it, Mama. And I'll have someone come and…" She trailed off as she looked around the desperate room. "I'll have someone help you clean this up, as well."

"Good," Mrs. Winchester said, and then motioned for the door even as she downed the entire glass she'd just poured for herself in one gulp. "Is there anything else or will you leave me in peace?"

Jane's nostrils flared. "Nothing else. But if you hear from Nora, please won't you contact me?"

Mrs. Winchester shrugged and poured herself another drink. Ripley could see Jane's eyes filling with tears, see her blinking them back desperately. He would not allow this wretched woman the gift of breaking her, so he took her hand and gently guided her from the room. The carriage hadn't moved, thankfully, so he waved to the driver, indicating he put out his cigar and get back into position. After he handed Jane up into the carriage, he pivoted to face her mother.

"Oy," he snapped, reverting back to less polite manners. "What kind of mother treats their girl like that? More to the point, what kind of monster doesn't care about their missing child?"

Mrs. Winchester fought to focus on his face and gripped the edge of the door a little to keep herself upright. "You don't know what I've been through."

He motioned his head toward Jane. "I know what you put *her* through. And what she is despite you. If you hear from Nora and don't contact her, I'll find out."

The other woman's nostrils flared. "A white knight, eh?" She snorted a bitter laugh. "Women like her, women like *us*…we burn white knights to the ground. You're already lost, so you can't do nothing to me."

With that she pivoted and flounced back into the house, slamming the door behind her.

Ripley had faced off in the ring with men bigger and stronger than him. He'd fought men who cheated, swung to kill, but it was this woman and her slings and arrows that slammed into Jane who made his hands shake. He smoothed them against his sides before he said a few words to the driver and got into the carriage.

Jane was bunched into the corner, looking out the opposite window. She didn't look at him when he closed the door behind himself and they blessedly rode away from the hell that was her mother's home. One thing he was certain of, though, was that they couldn't ride away from the consequences this day would leave.

Ripley hadn't spoken since they left her mother's home over an hour before. Jane had felt him watching her, occasionally he touched her hand, but as for words? He clearly had none.

But why would he? She had dragged him into the tawdry drama of her broken mother's home, strewn out all her horrible history for him to see. How could he say anything? How could he not see her differently as a result? It was probably for the best.

The carriage began to slow and she finally allowed herself to stop looking out the window and at him. It was only early evening, though she supposed he might be hungry. Not that she could eat. Her stomach turned just thinking about it.

"We'll stay here tonight," he said as he pulled the curtain back so she could see the fine inn where they had come.

She shook her head. "Stay here? What do you mean?"

He reached across to take her hand, his thumb smoothing along the webbing between her thumb and forefinger. "It's a long ride back still, the dark will make it dangerous. I don't think you're in any state to continue traveling, Janie. Rest will help. Food will help."

She stared at him, feeling the full weight of the kindness and care in his eyes. "I—oh."

"No arguments?" he teased, a little smile tilting the corners of his lips. "That's shocking."

She bent her head. "As if I could win any battle over you."

"You could win every battle," he said, then exited the carriage and offered a hand back for her.

She took it and stepped down on the crushed gravel of the drive. It was a lovely place, with a large gabled main house, a pretty stable and fresh, green grounds.

"If you'd like to stretch your legs, I'll fetch you after I've gotten our rooms arranged."

She nodded and felt his gaze on her as she walked down a well-tended path toward the garden behind the inn. The fading sunlight filtered through the trees, dancing off the green of the leaves and the rainbow beauty of the flowers. The images did bring her some measure of peace, but certainly not enough. All she could think about was the interaction with her mother. And worse, that she was no closer to finding her sister.

She shivered even though the air wasn't cold and sat down on a bench with a thump. There was a fountain in the middle of the garden and she focused on the never-ending flow of the water, the gurgling sounds of it falling.

How long she sat there, she didn't know. It must have been a while, though, for she jumped when she felt a hand on her shoulder. She jerked her head up and found Ripley waiting there. "Should I join you?"

She nodded. "You were so kind to leave me with my thoughts on the drive here, but I know I owe you a conversation. An...an apology for what happened at my mother's house."

He took a place next to her on the bench and stretched his muscular arm out on the back behind her. He hardly touched her, but she found herself wanting to lean into him, pull his arms around herself and forget everything.

That was foolish. Cruel to them both. He'd been kind, but there were limits and she knew she must be at the end of his now. Even if she wasn't, she wouldn't be like her mother and take advantage. Hurt him like she knew she could.

"You don't owe me any apology, Jane," he said. "You're no more responsible for your mother's behavior than you are for a stranger's. *I'm* sorry that you had to endure her callous disregard today and any day before this one."

She sighed. "She was never warm or loving. She lived a very hard life."

"Not an excuse," he said softly.

"Perhaps not, but an explanation," she said. "But she's definitely worse now. The drinking is part of that, but I think it goes deeper."

He nodded. "The state of the house was shocking."

"Well, hopefully whatever funds and assistance I arrange will help," she said, and shut her eyes. "Lord, the money."

"I know you put aside a healthy sum from your previous work. Does the shop do well enough to support assisting her?"

The image of the empty shop popped into her mind. The empty shop she despised, no matter how much she wanted to step into a more acceptable life. "It isn't your burden," she said.

He arched a brow. "It's not enough."

"Ripley," she whispered.

"Let me help," he said. "Let me arrange the funds and the assistance on your behalf."

She rose and paced away, feeling his gaze bore into her back. "That's outrageous. Kind, but out of the question. My mother thought you were my protector, but you aren't. You do not have any reason to waste money or any more time than you already have on—"

He got up and followed her, catching her arm and pivoting her back to face him. "You think I don't have a reason, Jane?"

She stared up into his face, rare emotion flashing in his dark eyes. Beautiful eyes. Soulful, warming, perfect eyes that could hold her steady and make her forget everything else but him.

She couldn't do that.

"You've done so much already." She extracted herself from his hands with a great deal of difficulty.

"I'm happy to do it," he insisted. "And considering we haven't found out anything about your sister expect that she isn't with your mother, we have a great deal more to do."

She blinked at him. "N-no. You were far too kind in your offer to bring me here and stand at my side, but you have a life back in London. A club and friends and—"

"It's not a question, Jane. I'm helping you and that's final." He folded his arms and his jacket tightened across his broad chest. "We can speak about it more later. Plot our next steps. For now, why don't you come upstairs? I'll help you get settled and you can rest."

Her instinct was to fight him. To push him away for both their sakes, but he wasn't wrong that she was tired. Physically, of course, it had been a long day and there had been no rest for her the prior night. But it was more a bone-deep exhaustion, something that went beyond a lack of sleep and burrowed into the weight of the world she'd borne for…well, she couldn't recall when she hadn't felt it on her shoulders, bowing her back.

"Very well," she sighed, and followed him into the inn. It was as pleasant inside as it was outside, clean and warm with smiling proprietors and guests chatting and eating.

Ripley took them past all that and up a wide staircase and down a hallway to a room. When she entered, she caught her breath. This had to be the largest chamber of the establishment, likely meant for very important guests as they passed through. The casement windows were cleaned to a shine so the gardens she'd been enjoying were easy to take in from the window seat.

A fire burned brightly in the large stone fireplace and a large bed was pressed against the wall across from it. On the other side of the room was a table and a screen where she assumed a bath was hiding.

"You spent too much. I'll never be able to repay you," she said.

He tilted his head. "I'm not asking for repayment. I want to take care of you, Jane. Whether that is taking you to visit your mother, continuing to search for your sister or getting you a decent room so that you may collapse as you look like you're ready to do after the last two days." He folded his arms again. "Now, tell me what you need."

She blinked. She couldn't recall the last time someone had asked her that. As a lightskirt, her life had been about anticipating and providing what others needed. She'd taken care of Esme when she was too innocent to know how to keep herself out of trouble. She'd protected her sister even though Nora despised her for it. Seeing her mother today had put her to mind of the long nights she'd spent as a child, trying to help the woman who'd raised her.

And this man asked what *she* needed.

"I don't know," she said. It was true. She'd pushed aside what she needed for so long it was hard to find the feeling of it, let alone the words.

"I can leave you," he said softly. "Let you rest a bit."

The idea of him walking away was instantly painful and she jerked toward him a step. "No!" she gasped out, and then shook her head. "It's not fair to ask, but would you just…just hold me for a moment?"

As she said it, she knew *that* was exactly what she needed. To feel the safety of his embrace, the steadiness of his presence. The world had an axis, after all, even when it spun out of control. She needed to find it.

His breath was shaky as he closed the remainder of the distance between them and folded his arms around her. She tilted her head to rest against the warm curve of his shoulder and breathed in the scent of him. Woodsy pine and leather, something masculine and soothing all at once. Suddenly she wanted to coat herself with that. Have it close by so she could pretend he was always with her.

They stood in the quiet like that for a few moments. He smoothed his hands against her hair, she clung to him. At first it was only the comfort she'd requested. But as she relaxed, the inevitable response of her body to his became very clear.

The heat of him wasn't *just* comforting. It was arousing. When his hands brushed her scalp, the sensitive skin tingled. When he shifted a little, she reveled in the strength of him. The thick solidness that she had often dreamed about since the first time she'd seen him, stripped half-naked in a ring, blood dripping down his forehead, eyes focused on his duty.

He let out a shuddering sigh and then began to step away, but she held to him. She lifted her face toward his and he looked at her. Now he wasn't breathing at all. She wasn't either.

"Please," she whispered.

His eyes fluttered shut. If nothing else, she knew he wanted her. That had always hung between them. Now she was testing his resolve. She was selfish enough she wanted to break it.

"Jane," he murmured, almost a plea.

"I want to forget for a while," she said, and stroked her fingers along the length of his spine. "With you."

CHAPTER 7

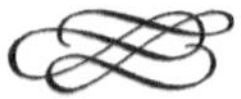

Ripley's breath was ragged as he stared down into Jane's face in the flickering firelight of the warm, quiet room. Perhaps there was some part of him that had always known it would come to this. That they'd opened a door when he kissed her the day before that couldn't be closed. That once they started, they'd be incapable of stopping the momentum of desire.

"I don't want to take advantage of your pain," he whispered.

She didn't answer with words. Instead she threaded her fingers through his hair and drew him down to her. Her breath was sweet on his lips, a whisper of her heat, and then she kissed him.

There was no resisting after that. Not when she drove her tongue against his, making a shivering sigh of desire and relief that made his whole body ache like he'd been in a fight. A losing fight, at that, though when she arched against him it was impossible to consider himself anything but a winner.

He cupped her closer, letting his fingers clench against the cotton of her gown, feeling the shape of her beneath the fabric. He couldn't help the low, possessive moan that followed and she bent her head back with a tremble.

He took the offering that created and pressed his mouth to her throat, tasting the delicate line there as she lifted against him, pulling herself ever closer. God, she tasted sweet, exactly as he'd imagined her skin would taste, dreamed about on nights when he woke rock hard and even his hand couldn't satisfy him.

He slid his mouth lower, across the exposed flesh above the bodice of her gown. He traced her collarbones, down to her chest, the top of her breasts. She whimpered, lifting again in silent plea.

He pushed her back and they fell against the bed together. He was on top of her and she squirmed beneath him, opening her legs as far as her pinned gown would allow, gripping one calf around him as she rocked beneath him.

Leaning back a fraction, he pushed his hand between them and found the line of buttons along the front of her gown. He flicked each one free, parting the dress, revealing her chemise beneath. It was sheer and lacy and he lifted his eyes to hers.

She smiled down at him. "I wasn't about to replace my under-things just because no one sees them anymore."

He dropped his head back to her chest. "Thank God for that," he murmured against her skin.

She pushed her dress aside and was working on the straps of her chemise when he closed his mouth around her nipple through the fabric. Immediately she jolted beneath him and let out a little cry that sounded like music to his ears. He sucked, loving the shape of her. Loving the sound of her pleasure.

Loving *her* even more than he had before, even more than he thought possible. He was lost now anyway, he might as well revel in every moment. Make memories to keep him warm later.

He slid his hands down her sides and she arched her back, offering herself up to him as he continued to lick her. She had the strap of her chemise off on one side now and she pulled it away, revealing the small, perfect globe of her breast.

"Christ," he muttered before he swirled his tongue around her nipple again, this time with nothing between him and the taste of her. She was panting as she ripped the chemise away entirely, baring herself to him. She pressed her breasts together and he flicked his tongue back and forth between them, teasing each one, stroking his tongue through the valley between them. She rocked beneath him as he did so, harsh breaths the only sound in the quiet room.

He drew lower, pulling the dress and chemise away as he dragged down her body, tossing them both over his shoulder when he could free her from them. Then he stood up and looked at her.

God, but she was perfect. So fucking perfect that he feared he'd never want any other person quite the same again. She would be the unattainable standard.

She watched him watch her for a brief moment and then she opened her legs. She wore pale cream stockings with a red pattern stitched through them. Her garters were the same red, stark and erotic against her pale skin.

And between the thighs where those garters were tied? A slick, pretty pussy he couldn't resist.

"What are you waiting for?" she murmured, reaching for him.

He chuckled. "I'm waiting because this is the point where I usually wake up."

Her eyes widened. "Are you saying you've had erotic dreams of me, Mr. Ripley?"

He nodded without breaking eye contact. "Every night since the first time I saw you, Jane."

Her lip trembled in response. "What did you dream you'd do to me? When you didn't wake up at this most inopportune time?"

He untied his cravat, shrugged from his jacket, stripped his shirt. He tugged off one boot, then the other before he stepped toward her.

"Feast," he growled, and pressed his hands into her thighs. She gasped as he bent between them, burying his head there and drawing a deep whiff of the sweet smell of her desire. When he stroked his tongue across her, the taste was even better. She jolted and her fingers came into his hair, holding him against her as she began to rock against his tongue.

They worked together at pleasing her. He tasted every inch of her slick sex, then put his focus on her clitoris. She arched it in time to his tongue, moaning and gasping so he knew what made her ache. Time slipped away, meaningless as he brought her closer and closer to the edge of madness.

When she found it, he smiled against her, reveling in the way she twitched and fluttered while he sucked her clitoris with merciless drive. He wanted to draw all the pleasure from her. He wanted her to be liquid and boneless beneath him. He wanted her hoarse from her cries. The same gorgeous cries that echoed in the room. Probably echoed in the hallway for the other guests to hear. But who gave a damn? This moment was theirs and no one else could ever take it.

When she went limp on the bed, when her hands fell away from his hair, when the jolting of her body calmed to mere flutters, he lifted his head and looked at her.

She was pink from pleasure, her dark blue gaze foggy from release. Gone was the pain from the day, gone was the fear for her sister. For a moment, at least, he had freed her from all that. And it would be enough.

Only when he began to roll away from her, she caught his shoulder. "Where do you think you're going?"

He smiled. "Did I fail to please?"

"You pleased beyond anything I've ever experienced," she said. "But you're not finished. Not by half."

She was temptation embodied, but he did his best to resist her. "You've been through a great deal today and I—"

She sat up, wrapping her arms around his shoulders, forcing him to be face to face with her. "Campbell Ripley, if you don't fuck me right now I will challenge you to a duel at dawn."

His brows rose and he laughed. "A fight to the death?"

"Just a little one," she whispered, and then kissed him deeply all over again and pulled him back down over her.

～

In her vast experience, Jane hadn't met many men who gave a damn about her pleasure, let alone her emotions. But Ripley was not like other man. Not like any man. Here he had her splayed out naked beneath him, still quivering from the most powerful orgasm she'd ever experienced, and he was ready to back away to give her respite. Even though she could feel the heavy steel of his cock pressing to her belly. He wanted her and he would refuse his own needs for hers.

What a thing to have her well-being mean more than someone else's wants. Only what she needed, what would make her better, was him. Him inside of her. Hers, even if it was just for tonight.

She wasn't about to let him walk away from that. From her. From this.

She wrapped her thighs around his hips and he pushed against her, his cock nudging her pussy even though he was still wearing his trousers. She nipped his lower lip and he growled, his expression growing even more heated, feral. He looked like he did when he was in the ring, focused and powerful. When he kissed her, there was no more hesitation or gentleness. He devoured her, sucking her tongue, driving inside.

She glided her hands down his sides, shivering at the muscular thickness of his body. How many times had she wondered what he'd feel like? He was better than any imagining.

She crossed her hands over his flat stomach, tracing muscle with her palm, and notched her fingers into the waistband of his trousers. His kiss deepened further, moans lost in her mouth, as she unfastened the fall front and let him bounce free into her palm.

She flattered her other hand against his chest and pushed him back so she could look between their bodies. Look at him. He was thick, hard, the impressive length of him curling toward his stomach in a proud display of desire.

She stroked him, loving how he dropped his head back with a grunt of pleasure. This man was always in control. He was powerful and steady. She wanted to be the one who made him tremble, turned him animal.

She smiled up at him, knowing she was being wicked, watching his pupils dilate until his eyes were almost entirely black. "I want this," she whispered. "Let me have it, Ripley."

He caught her thighs, his fingers digging in, and tugged her to the edge of the bed. She sat up, winding her arms around his neck, tracing the muscles of his shoulders with the very edge of her nails. He spread her wide, stepping between her legs. When he kissed her, he put his hand between her thighs, stroked his fingers across her wet sex. He opened her, fitting the head of his cock against her. She lifted and he glided deep inside.

She shuddered with the feel of him, the weight of him, moving through her. He seated himself fully and then drew his face back, meeting her eyes.

"God, you feel good," he said, his voice low and rough in the quiet. "I want to take you hard and fast, but I don't want to hurt you."

She smiled. "I'm not some virgin made of glass. Take me hard and fast. Show me how much you wanted me all this time. Let me show you the same."

He cupped the back of her neck, his fingers teasing into her hair. She tilted her face, watching him as he withdrew a little from her body, then thrust forward again. The slap of their bodies meeting made her arch as pleasure ripped through her. How could he do that so easily? Was it just wanting this so long that made her weak? Or was it him?

She feared she knew that answer.

But she pushed it aside and ground against him, squeezing tight as he thrust again, again, harder and faster each time. His mouth found hers and there was nothing but sensation as he pounded into her, one hand cupping her backside, the other holding her head, taking her with his tongue and his cock at the same time.

She pushed her hand between their tightly pressed bodies, brushing her fingers against the wet length of him when he withdrew once more. He jolted faster at the sensation, his teeth scraping her lower lip with just enough pressure that she gasped.

She moved her hand against her clitoris, riding her fingers and his cock all at once. The pleasure mounted, edging even higher this time as she gripped against him. When she came she buried her mouth into his shoulder, crying out his name.

Well, she *tried* to call out his name. His first name, but all she could manage was a broken, "Cam—Cam—Cam!" as her body flexed out of control.

He cried out with her and then withdrew, the heat of him splashing against her skin, leaving his mark on her even if it would be wiped away far too soon.

She collapsed back, dragging him beside her. His arms came around her, their panting breaths echoing together in the warmth and peace of that room. Peace. What a concept. One she'd not had much in her life and yet she recognized it somehow, lying in this man's arms, his breath stirring her hair whenever he pressed a gentle kiss to her temple.

Only there couldn't be peace. Even if her life allowed it, her current situation didn't. Her thoughts and focus had to be on Nora. This was a brief respite, nothing more.

"If my sister didn't go to my mother..." she whispered.

She felt him stiffen and then he eased up on an elbow to look down into her face. "You said she stopped writing some time ago. Do you know her friends?"

She shook her head. "No. I didn't want what I am...was...to taint her, so I didn't visit. I never met any girls she might be close to at the school. The ones who might be helping her, or know more about who might have taken her."

"Then it sounds like our next step is to go to the school. How far is it?"

She sat up. "Ripley—"

He touched her face. "I liked it when you called me Cam. When you're naked in a bed beside me, I want you to call me that."

How could a man be so hard, with his slightly bent nose, with the scar across his eyebrow, with the stern line of his mouth and the harsh ridge of his jaw…and yet be so gentle at the same time?

"Cam," she tried, testing it and finding she liked it, too. Liked having that special name for him like he did for her when he sometimes called her Janie. She fought to retain focus on the matters at hand. "I said it to you in the garden—I can't put you into this mess any more than you have been."

"You aren't *putting* me anywhere," he insisted. "I'm not a man to be *put*."

"No, I suppose not," she agreed. "But—"

"I'm going with you," he interrupted. "And I'm finished arguing about it."

Now his face really was hard, a reflection of his apparently immovable statement. And though she knew she ought to fight him more, force the issue, the idea of him being by her side as she searched, by her side if she found out the terrible things that haunted her, that was a relief. She had never needed anyone in her life, but she needed him right now.

"Fine," she said. "She has been going to the Knightly Seminary for Young Women. It's in the country about two days north of London."

"So we'll need to go back through the city either way," he said. "Good. That will give you a chance to gather some things for the road and let me arrange for a more permanent travel situation."

"Yes, that makes sense," she said. "I hadn't even thought of it."

"See?" he said with a sad smile. "You do need me after all."

"I never questioned that I needed you, Ripley. Cam." She touched his face and then let her fingers glide down. He shivered, but caught her hand and lifted it to his lips.

"Do you want to go downstairs and eat? Or rest alone?"

She shook her head. "No. No, what I want is right here."

He held her gaze steady and then pulled her in for another kiss, shifting onto his back and tugging her over him. She let all other thoughts drift away, lost herself in him, knowing that at some point that decision would come back to haunt her.

CHAPTER 8

Ripley had never returned to his own room the previous night. Staying in Jane's bed, sharing food with her by the fire as she wore nothing but his shirt, waking up with her in his arms… it was like every dream come true.

They hadn't spoken of it, though. Of what their night together meant. While they rode back to London, she'd asked him to read more from his novel, which didn't allow for questions. Perhaps for the best, as he wasn't certain he'd like the answers. If she pushed him away, he would have to honor that.

Now they pulled up before her shop and sat staring at each other for a moment. He'd asked the driver not to open the door, so they had as long as he'd like to stay in the bubble of what they'd shared.

She reached across the carriage and took his hand. Certainly not the first time she'd done so, but the first time this day and the action carried more weight now that they'd touched in far more intimate ways.

"I know you've firmly shut the door on this conversation," she began. "But I must say it one more time: I don't want to take advantage of your kindness."

"You can take advantage any time," he replied. He'd meant to sound teasing, but it wasn't. She heard it too, for she bent her head with a little sigh.

"Should we do this?" she asked.

"Find your sister?"

"No." She lifted her gaze to his. "We've stayed away for so long, Ripley. We've fought this pull between us."

He swallowed. This was the conversation he'd waited for and yet he felt no joy with it. Not when she appeared so concerned. "If you don't want to—"

"No, I didn't say that," she interrupted.

He smiled a little at how swiftly she said it. All that love for her rose up in him, stronger now because they'd acted on the attraction. Because he knew what it felt to join with her in the most intimate way. He would take the pain that would come for this. Pain was sometimes worth the moment before.

"I'm here, Jane," he said. "I'll be here however you need me. When it comes to what happened between us last night, if you want to leave it as a night of passion, one that I'll never forget, I won't push. If you want to crawl into my bed every night we're searching for your sister and let me ease your troubles for a few hours, I'm happy to do that, as well. More than happy."

She worried her lip and it made him want to nip it like he had so many times the night before. He lived for the way that made her hiss in her breath with pleasure.

"You don't have to decide right now," he assured her, and then he opened the carriage door and stepped out to help her down. When her feet were firmly back on the ground, he said, "I'll let you know how the arrangements are going as I progress during the day."

"Yes, thank you. Please keep a list of your expenses. At least let me try to cover them."

He ignored that request because he had no intention of honoring it. Instead he asked, "Have you thought about going to Esme about this? I'm sure she and Delacourt could be of help."

Her lips pinched and he could see her feelings. Her fears were far too plain on her face. "I…no. Not yet at any rate. If I cannot do this on my own, I'll trade on our friendship. But for now, let me keep them out of it."

"Of course," he said. "Whatever you think is best, Jane."

"I'll be ready in the morning," she said.

For a moment he thought she might kiss him right here on the walkway in front of her store. She leaned a little toward him, her lips upturned. But then she caught herself and turned away, dashing to the door where she slipped inside and left him alone.

"Take me back to the club, please," he told the driver before he got back into the vehicle and settled in. As they rumbled across the city, he stared across at where she'd been sitting. He could still smell her in the air. He could almost still feel her warmth.

But amidst all that, past all the memories of her body flexing around his, he could also perfectly picture her terror. She might need his body in order to soothe her worries, but she also needed him to be on his guard, be at his best so that they might find her sister.

If they couldn't, he already knew it would be devastating to her. Destructive. He didn't want to watch her go through that pain, one he couldn't help with. He knew that feeling far too well.

They rolled to a stop before the club and he thanked the driver as he got out. He strode through the doors to find the familiar sounds of men sparring echoing in the room around him. As he had expected, all was well after Brentwood's short reign as leader of the club. A few of the men training waved to him as he came in, but most simply continued their punches and blocks.

He searched for Brentwood and found him in the back of the hall, standing with the Earl of Kirkwood. The earl was a reasonably good fighter, despite his rank. He was also friends with Delacourt and Ramsbury, so Ripley would have to be careful with what was said. At this point Jane didn't want the help of her powerful friends and he wasn't going to push it.

"Ah, Ripley," Kirkwood said with a wide smile and a hand

extended to shake. "We missed you this morning at the usual practice."

From some men, Ripley might have bristled, but he could tell the statement was meant truthfully, not as some barely veiled dig. "I apologize for my absence. I had some personal business to attend to. I fear I must steal Brentwood away, assuming you two are finished with your conversation."

Kirkwood inclined his head. "We are. Best of luck with whatever is happening. Good day, gentlemen."

As the earl stepped away, Ripley motioned Brentwood back to his office and shut the door.

"And so you are back," Brentwood said, his tone noncommittal.

"I assume all went well in my absence."

Brentwood nodded. "Just the usual. Toffs doing their practice, trying to show off for one another on the whole. Some of the professionals getting ready for arranged fights. There's a new one you'll probably want to look at, he has potential. Should I arrange a meeting?"

"Yes," Ripley said. He always tried to see the ones he thought he could help. Just like in the lightskirt trade, there were too many bad actors in the fighting game. At least if Ripley assisted the young ones, he knew they wouldn't be taken advantage of. "But not this week. I won't be here."

Brentwood held his stare a moment and then nodded. "I see. More business with Miss Kendall, I assume."

Ripley shifted before he meant to do so and realized he'd just moved into a fighting stance. Probably because he felt protective of Jane and he knew now what she thought Brentwood's feelings were about her. "Yes." He folded his arms. "She believes you don't like her."

Brentwood let out a long sigh. "Of course I like her. She's impossible not to like. I admire her strength and her loyalty to Esme."

"All that is true," Ripley said. "And yet I sense a but."

"But…" The hesitation that came before the next words felt like an eternity. "But you love her, mate."

Ripley stepped back and deposited himself on the edge of his worn desk. He stared at Brentwood, a man he'd known since his fighting days. He was the closest person he had to a best friend, but they rarely spoke of personal matters. It wasn't in either of their natures. And Ripley had spent a lifetime trying to cover up his emotions. He was very good at it.

Except now it seemed he hadn't been.

"Have I stunned the Dragon into silence?" Brentwood asked softly. "Or are you just considering where to punch me?"

"The Dragon was known for his strong silence," Ripley said with a flinch. "I'm not him anymore."

"I was sparring with Walter Mandy earlier. He still can't keep that left up. He's going to get his bell rung if he fights anyone with a brain."

Ripley wrinkled his brow in confusion. Was Brentwood changing the subject to be kind? "I'll remind him when I'm in the ring with him next."

"I'm sure you will." Brentwood folded his arms. "What do you say when a fighter has a persistent weakness?"

"It's dangerous," Ripley said. "You need to train it out because it's a tell that becomes too easy to read for any opponent. A way past the guard that could end you."

"She's your weakness, mate. Far larger than any you had when you swung your fists for a living."

Pushing off the desk, Ripley turned away to stare at the disorganized papers stacked there. He didn't see them, he just didn't want to be so exposed while he pondered that statement. "Perhaps she is," he admitted. "Are you saying I need to train her out?"

"Not necessarily. Not if you don't feel it's dangerous."

Ripley choked out a laugh. Of course it was dangerous to love Jane. It was hopeless, most likely. He'd always known that with every wall she erected to keep them from being close. Making love to her hadn't changed that, just made it all the more painful.

"But you do need to know the weakness exists so that you can protect yourself."

Ripley faced him and forced a tight smile. "You needn't worry about me," he said, though he wasn't certain that was true. "Just keep the club going."

"I will."

"And if you think this new one you talked about is worthy, offer him a place with our others. I trust you."

Brentwood's brows lifted at the suggestion Ripley had never made before. It meant something and they both knew it. "I will."

Ripley gathered some things. "I'll update you on my timeline and if I need any assistance. Your carriage is back, thank you again for the loan. I'll let one for the trip, as I don't know how long we'll be gone and I don't want to deprive you. I need to go arrange that and some other things now."

He clapped Brentwood on the shoulder and then headed for the door.

"Be careful," his friend said as he reached it.

Ripley gripped the jamb and turned back with a wide smile. "I never am."

Then he stepped out and back through the club toward the unknown. But Brentwood's words rang in his mind. He feared they would for a long time to come.

CHAPTER 9

The carriage Ripley showed up with the following morning wasn't the same one he'd come with before. After Jane settled into its worn leather seats and they began to roll away toward Copperworth, the village where her sister's school was located, she asked, "Where did you get this rig from?"

"I let it."

She caught her breath. "Ripley! The cost."

"Stop," he said softly. "I have the money."

She huffed out a breath. He might dismiss his help as nothing, but it wasn't. She owed him far more than she could ever repay. All her life she had tried to never be in that position. She'd have to find a way to even the scales between them.

A flash entered her mind of his mouth between her legs, of his cock driving into her, but she pushed it away. She didn't want their passion to be transactional.

She cleared her throat and he arched a brow, as if anticipating her argument. Instead, she asked, "Do you think I'm being right in the way I'm pursuing my sister?"

"How do you mean?"

"There's a part of me that wants to drive through the night, scream through every town, asking after her. And yet we're doing this in a measured manner."

He nodded. "I see. I suppose we could push horses and employees and ourselves to the brink. That's always an option. But this is a fight, Jane, and I'm the expert on that matter."

"There's no denying that." She pursed her lips. "So what does the *expert* think?"

"In a fight, it's better to meter one's response. To measure strikes before letting them fly. At this point, we don't know enough to go wild. We're keeping ourselves from breaking before we need strength."

She considered that. "I understand. So…how do we do this next part of the fight?"

"We go to the school and question that horrid headmistress who wrote you such an awful message about your sister's disappearance. It's easier to dismiss one's duty by post than in person and she might know more than she wished to share."

"And if she doesn't? Or if she won't?"

His lips thinned like the idea was upsetting. "Then we talk to every schoolmaster and girl who attended lessons with her. All her friends, people in the village who might have encountered her. Anyone who knew Nora."

Her breath caught at that turn of phrase and she gripped her hands in her lap as fear rose up in her chest and nearly choked her. "Knows," she corrected, her voice shaking.

His expression fell and he lunged to grab her hands. "I'm sorry. Knows. I'm sorry, Jane. I didn't mean to say it like that."

She stared into his eyes. He was so good at hiding his feelings. When she'd first met him, first come to know him, she could never tell what he thought. But over time, she'd begun to see his tells. Little twitches and swiftly buried flashes of emotion. Normally it was a fun game she played for herself.

Today it wasn't. She saw what he wouldn't say and she sighed. "I-I realize the worst might happen, could have already happened, to my sister." She set her shoulders back, tried to stiffen her resolve by straightening her spine. "I don't want you to think me a fool."

"Jane, the last thing I'd ever see you as is a fool."

They were both quiet for a moment as the warmth of that comment eased her a little. He did that so easily, it was almost overpowering.

She drew in a breath. "Do you have siblings?"

He shifted and drew his hands away. "I had a sister. She died at birth."

"I'm sorry. How old were you?"

"About ten," he said, and smiled at her. "We were both the much older sibling, it seems, even if I was only that for the span of a breath."

She nodded. They had so much in common, really. Hard lives punctuated with pain, but also a resilience she often leaned on. She watched him do the same. But she also knew from experience that sometimes cracks appeared in that shell. Then it was precarious to pretend strength. Did that happen to him? Was it possible he sometimes broke?

"I suppose her death," he continued slowly, as if he had to be careful around this topic, "was just another piece of kindling on the fire of my mother's sorrow. And I always wonder what that little girl would have been like. What she would be like now at nineteen. How we would have taken care of each other when our mother died."

"I think she would have been strong," she said. "Like you."

He smiled briefly. "What's Nora like?"

She shook her head. "I hardly know anymore thanks to the estrangement I mentioned to you before."

"When she was young, then. Before her misunderstanding of your motives drove you apart."

She closed her eyes and pictured her sister with her dark blonde curls and her snapping blue eyes that were so like Jane's own. She thought of her bubbly laugh and her constant chatter.

"Sweet," she whispered at last. "Witty. God, that child was smart. *Is* smart. She taught herself to read when she was six."

"But not you?" he asked.

She started, but then recalled she had told him she had only recently learned to read when he offered to share his book with her. "No. I had too much to do to take time to learn."

He frowned. "You mean you took all your time protecting her. Protecting your mother."

She nodded. "But that allowed Nora to be carefree for so much longer. Any sacrifice was worth that."

"I'm not sure I agree," he said, stretching a long arm out along the back of the seat beside him. Putting her to mind of when he'd done that in the garden of the inn a couple of days before. "But I'm biased. So how did you learn later?"

She hesitated. "Esme taught me."

His brow wrinkled and she prayed he wouldn't ask why. She didn't want to say or be forced to hide that she had learned to read because he'd written her little notes. Words that were so precious that she wanted them all for herself, that she collected and pored over time and again.

And to her relief, he didn't ask. He merely nodded. "I have a great deal of respect for that, Jane. Now, if it's not rude, I'm going to try to sleep a bit, I think. I was kept up by most pleasant activities two nights ago and by preparing for our journey last night."

"I can entertain myself," she said.

"We'll stop along the road in a few hours to break our fast and rest the horses. I'll be awake before then."

He slouched down in the carriage, leaned his head against the wall near the window and shut his eyes. She found herself watching him, counting his breaths, noting the shifts as he went from alertness to relaxation to sleep. Seeing how his expression changed when it was calm. She noted it all and collected it in the vault of knowledge she had about this man.

Then she looked outside to the scenery along their route and focused her attention there. Focused on where she was going so she wouldn't disrupt herself with dreams of what might have been in another life.

~

It had been a long day of travel and Ripley's body felt it. After his nap and their break for food, they had read more. It was a way to separate themselves from the deeper conversations they'd had earlier about family and responsibility, but he also enjoyed sharing the book with her. He loved watching her eyes widen with delight at the adventures he recounted.

But now he set the book aside as the late afternoon bled into evening. Darkness was beginning to set in outside, dimming the light from the windows. "We'll stop for the night soon."

She nodded. "Yes. I know without a moon it would be too dangerous to continue."

"When we do…" he said slowly, feeling nervous, almost like a green boy.

She blinked at the halting sentence. "When we do?" she encouraged.

"I—should I ask the innkeeper for one room or two?" he asked. "There is no pressure either way and if you want privacy or you've changed your mind about what we shared before, I won't mention it again."

She looked down at her hands, clenching and unclenching them in her lap. Her lips had thinned and her cheeks were flushed when she looked up at him.

"I'm not a mincing virgin," she said at last. "Sex is a physical need, or it always has been, whether I was paid for it or enjoyed it… or both, occasionally. But it was different with you."

He sucked in a breath. "Oh?"

"It was better." She met his eyes. "And I won't lie and try to pretend that it wasn't. You'd see through me at any rate. You always do. Being with you helps me forget about my fear for a little while. So, if you want to share a room with me, I won't turn that down."

A pressure Ripley hadn't fully realized was pushing down on him lifted the instant she said those beautiful words. A rush of desire and love moved through him instead, washing away reason and restraint. He knew, even as he leaned forward, that was exactly what Brentwood meant when he said Ripley's love for Jane was dangerous. That it was a weakness he had to be aware of so he wouldn't be injured by it, or worse.

He knew that and he still pushed it away, cupped her cheeks and kissed her. It hadn't even been a full day since the last time he'd done that, and yet it felt like a lifetime. Like he'd been parched in a desert and now she was water. She gripped his forearms with a gasping moan and there was no stopping this heat between them now.

He dropped to his knees before her, pressing her back against the carriage wall, cupping her against him with one hand, tracing her jawline with the other. She lifted into him so there was no space, no breath. It was only them and this and the inevitable conclusion to fire meeting oil in such a combustible way.

It was only that the rap on the carriage door that stopped them. They both startled apart and Jane glanced at the door. She looked at him and then she laughed. For a moment he saw the wicked, playful side of her that had been muted since she took over the shop, certainly since she heard her sister was missing.

"You are a distraction…Cam," she murmured.

His stomach flipped when she used that name. No one called him that. Even Campbell was incredibly rare. Esme only used it to tweak him like a sibling might. That Jane used the name for the moments when they were alone, when he was hers in body and soul, gave it weight.

"You'll moan that name next," he promised, and opened the door. "Place a wager on it, Janie."

She giggled and slipped from the carriage first. She stretched her back and looked up at the inn they'd reached as he joined her. A gentleman in what felt like an explosion of tweed approached with a wide smile. His Scottish accent was almost incomprehensible as he said, "Aye, there you be. Welcome to the Piper's Rest. Taron Fergus at your service. Will you be needin' a room or just a meal?"

"A room for my..." Ripley paused and glanced down at Jane at his side. They'd never see these people again, but he wasn't about to say anything that might make Jane be seen as less. "My wife and I."

She drew in a sharp breath when he said it. He had to fight not to do the same. Jane as his wife. There was a thought. One he pushed away.

"And one for our driver, who's taking care of the stable needs at present."

"Excellent, excellent," the innkeeper said. "Let me see what's available and I'll escort you up meself."

He hustled to the low table with a handful of numbered cubbies behind it. As he looked through them for the room he'd choose, Jane glanced up at Ripley. "You didn't have to say that."

"What?" he asked, even though he knew full well what she meant.

"That I'm your wife," she whispered. "I've been to an inn with a gentleman lover before."

He nodded. "Of course you have. And there was nothing wrong with that. We both made our money from our bodies, there's no shame in such a thing. But I know it makes some look at you differently. Plus, you aren't in the trade anymore. You're a respectable lady."

She snorted. "Hardly. You're far more respectable than I am."

He glared at her playfully. "Oh, Jane, are we about to have our first quarrel? Fighting over who has the dubious distinction of respectability?"

She laughed and it was like music. "I wouldn't dare paint you with such an awful brush. I do apologize."

"Yes, you'll have to make it up to me when we get upstairs and—"

He turned his attention back to the bustling innkeeper. "Ah, Mr. Fergus. Do you have accommodation?"

"I do. A fine room. Follow me."

They did so, trailing after the man. After a few steps, Jane slipped her hand into the crook of Ripley's elbow and a full shiver wracked him at the touch. She'd held his cock in her hand and yet this felt more intimate on some level.

They reached the room and Mr. Fergus let them in. He drew the curtains open with some flourish, even though there was only darkness outside by now, and tossed a log on the low fire. And all the time he talked and talked about the room and the inn and the supper to be had in the dining hall from eight to eleven that night.

Ripley watched Jane the entire time the poor man made his speeches. She was nodding and kindly answering his questions, but every once in a while she shot a playful look toward Ripley. Saucy, he thought some might call it.

"May I help with anything else?" Mr. Fergus said at last.

"Oh no, sir, you've been most kind," Jane said. "My dear husband and I are very tired from our long journey, I fear. We'll take some rest before we indulge in the sumptuous food you've described so eloquently."

"Very good, very good, madam." The innkeeper stepped into the hallway and pivoted back as if to speak further.

"Good evening," Jane said sweetly, then shut the door and turned the key to lock it. She faced Ripley slowly and leaned back with a wicked grin. "I thought he'd stay forever. That we'd have to invite him to play."

Ripley laughed. "He isn't exactly my type in men, but if it made you happy."

There was no reaction from her at that statement beyond another deeply wicked smile. She stepped toward him, hips twitching in the most fascinating way. She wrapped her arms around his neck, her breasts flattening as her mouth lifted just to his lips without touching them.

"What would make me happy is to be very naked and very alone with you."

He wobbled. The first time they'd been to bed together, it had felt deep. Important. Changing. Tied to her dark emotions, an escape.

But this…this felt light. Playful. Passionate. He slid a hand into the bun at the nape of her neck and dragged his fingers across her scalp to tilt her face closer. "Then we're halfway there. Seems it's time to get down to the other half. With great pleasure."

CHAPTER 10

Jane's mind had been tangled with fear all day as they traveled, but Ripley so easily changed that. He gave her the space and permission to relax, to let go. Perhaps it was because he never minimized her fear, he never threatened to use it against her, so she knew he would still be there when she picked it all back up again.

That wasn't how it normally was with lightskirts. Gentlemen, even those who took a lady as their officially protector, often didn't want to see or hear anything but the good. The rest had to be pushed down. She'd done so all her life.

Except with the man standing before her now, his mouth brushing hers. She could feel his wicked smile against her lips, like this could be fun. She needed fun right now.

With a smile, she pushed back out of his arms. He released her with only the arch of his scarred brow. One more thing that made him singular. He never forced or pushed, even though he was so much bigger than she was, he could have taken anything he wanted. But he never did. He never would.

Lifting her hands to the buttons along the bodice of her simple gown, she met his eyes. Slowly, she unfastened herself, carefully parting the fabric of her dress to reveal the chemise beneath little by little. He smiled as he realized what she was doing and shifted his weight, putting his hands behind his back.

She lowered the gown from one shoulder. "Why do you put your hands back there?"

His chuckle was low and smoky. "Because if I don't, I might not be able to control myself. And I'm very much enjoying the show."

"Ahhh." She lowered the other side of the gown and let it bunch around her hips. "That's a good idea, because for what I have in mind, I very much want to be in control. In fact…"

She shoved the dress away, gave him a brief moment to look her up and down in her chemise, and then came toward him. She touched the cravat tied lazily at his throat. "Do you mind if I use that for a much more interesting purpose?"

He tilted his head. "I can only imagine what that wicked mind of yours has planned. Certainly. But only if you remove it yourself."

"I wouldn't have it any other way."

She stepped up, giving him her best coquettish look. The one she had perfected after years of being the lover of many a man. His smile remained and it reached his eyes, making them sparkle. For a moment she faltered, because to be this close to him when he shone was…remarkable.

"Or do you need help?" he asked.

"No." She shook her head. "I'm just enjoying every moment."

He inclined his head as if to encourage her to continue. She pressed her hands against his stomach and unfastened the few buttons on his coat. She slid her fingers inside, tracing the muscles she could feel even beneath his waistcoat and shirt. He shifted and his playful smile fell, but he still didn't stop her or take her power.

She flattened her hands and slid them up his chest, memorizing every twitch of his body, every line of him. When she reached the cravat, she tangled her fingers in the fabric and gave a gentle tug so that he bent slight to allow her access.

His mouth was close to hers now, but she didn't kiss him. She teased him though as she unknotted the cravat without even looking at it. She let her lips brush but never fully meet his, she let them whisper along his jawline.

His breath increased when she did and he shifted again. She would wager if she looked at his hands behind his back now they would be clenched tightly, locked in a fight to keep himself from touching her.

She drew the cravat around and around until it fell away from him, then she wrapped the long length around her palms before she moved around behind him, brushing his body with hers.

As she suspected, his hands were locked together, his wrists close, just as she wanted them. Gently she touched them, giving him a hint of what she would do in case he wanted to refuse her. He didn't, though when she wrapped the cravat around them once, he sucked in a shaky breath.

She wrapped the fabric a few more times, loosely enough that it wouldn't hurt him, then knotted the loops into place before she pressed herself to his back and kissed his shoulder through the layers of his clothes. "And now you're mine."

"I could rip that cravat in half, you know," he said, his voice dark now. Erotic.

"You could," she said as she moved around him, keeping her body flush to his. "Easily, I'm sure. But you won't. Because you want what I'm going to do. So you'll be very good and let me."

"You're a wicked one," he said.

"Just like you like me, I think." She pushed the jacket wide and unfastened the waistcoat beneath, then the shirt so that half his chest was revealed.

"Didn't think that through, did you?" he teased. "I'll have half my clothes on at least."

"Oh no, I thought it through perfectly," she insisted as she pushed him back toward the settee before the fire. "I want you to be undone, messy, wrinkled as you sprawl out on that settee."

She shoved and he sat back, shifting to allow space for his tied hands. She grabbed for a pillow and dropped it between his feet on the rug.

"I want you to look down and see your cock in my mouth while you're fully clothed." She took to her knees on the cushion and pushed his thighs wider so that he was sprawled there. "There's something so lewd about it, isn't there? Something so wicked that you are almost proper except that you're watching me do such a thing."

She flicked the buttons on his fly front open and lowered it, letting his cock, which was already fully hard, bounce free. He grunted rather than answered her, his legs flexed as she reached out a finger and traced his length.

"Watch me, Cam," she whispered, and smiled when he jolted. She liked that. She liked all of this. "Watch me take your control lick by lick, suck by suck."

He nodded jerkily and stared as she lowered her mouth to him. She examined the fine cock displayed for her enjoyment. He truly was a specimen, and she already knew how much pleasure he could give. But how much could he take?

She darted out her tongue and gave the length of him a teasing lick. He bit out a breath and his body tensed. She smiled up at him. "I'd wager you want to rip that flimsy little cravat in half."

He nodded wordlessly.

"But you won't," she taunted, and bent her head to lick him again, this time with more pressure. He tasted clean and a little salty. She licked again, and this time she held back a moan.

Oh, this was going to be as much a test of her own control as his. And she was more than ready to pass or fail. Either way, she'd get everything she wanted.

Jane swirled her tongue around the sensitive head of his cock and Ripley shuddered from the intense pleasure. Her mouth was so hot, so wet, and she was very good at what she was doing that he feared he might forget everything but this.

Only he didn't like that she felt she had to *force* him to do her bidding. So as she sucked him, he worked at the knot behind his back. It wasn't tied very tightly. She clearly hadn't wanted to damage him, just keep him from forcing her hand.

But he had no intention of doing that.

When she gripped him, sliding her hand up and down his length while she rolled her tongue around him once more, he couldn't hold back his moan. His fingers faltered in his work and pleasure streaked up his length, through his balls, his veins, dancing along his skin.

His reaction seemed to spur her on. She watched him, dark blue eyes locked with his as she licked and stroked, back and forth, her tongue leaving wetness for her hand to roll through so that the way was lubricated. He found himself lifting a little, meeting her strokes and finally her mouth as she took him inside and sucked.

Stars exploded in his vision, but he continued to loosen the knot. He freed it at last, but didn't draw his hands from behind his back. He would prove he was capable of allowing her what she needed, whether that was giving or receiving pleasure.

She took him deeper into her throat, deeper still, until she had the full length of him in her mouth. Her tongue beat out a rhythm as she pumped over him, stroked over him, and built him, on and on, toward release.

"Fuck," he moaned, knocking his head back on the settee cushion. "That feels so good, Janie."

She moaned against him, the vibration adding to the sensation. She had built his pleasure brick by brick, lick by lick, but he was beginning to feel the edges of it fray. He would come soon, there would be no stopping it. And he so wanted to have it be after he watched her shatter around him.

He tried to focus. "I'm going to spend," he said. "And if you want me to shatter and give you every drop, I will. But I want to be inside you, Jane. I want to bury deep into you while you moan and cry out my name. I want to feel you come and watch you go weak with pleasure.

She lifted her head from his cock and braced her hands on his thighs. "I-I want that, too," she whispered. "I thought making you come would be enough, but I'm wild with you, Cam. Let me untie you."

He pulled his hands from behind his back and held them up to show her they were already unbound. "No need."

She rocked back a little. "Wait…you untied yourself? When?"

"A while ago." He caught her elbows and drew her up. She settled her legs on either side of him and together they shoved her chemise up around her stomach. She wore nothing beneath but her stockings and she gasped as he reached between them and stroked his cock along the already wet heat of her.

"You don't have to force me," he said, "in order to trust me, Jane. If you ask, I'll always do as you need. As you wish. I promise."

She blinked down at him, her gaze suddenly foggy and filled with emotion. She cupped his cheeks and leaned in to kiss him as her body opened to him and he slid inside gently. She groaned into his mouth and then whispered, "You may be the only man I'd ever believe that from."

"Good."

He caught her hips and helped her rock. She ground against him, her hands pressing into his shoulders, her legs gripping around his thighs through his trousers. And she was right. There was something lascivious about being spread out on this settee with all his clothes on, being ridden to the edge of madness. Something he never wanted to end, even though the sharp edge of release was right there.

It seemed it was for her too. Her strokes became wilder, faster. Her moans and groans began to echo on the air. She arched her back and her body began to grip his in harsh, rippling waves. She keened, tears coming down her cheeks, cries incoherent with pleasure.

His own pleasure was uncontainable now, streaking through his cock, burning through his veins, making him more animal than man. He shifted her onto her back, pulling her leg up over his thigh, and took her in long, heavy strokes as she continued to arch and wail beneath him. He held out as long as he could, savoring every moment, but at last it was too much and he withdrew. Her fingers tangled with his and together they pumped him to completion between them before he collapsed down over her, pressing his mouth to her neck and her shoulders, her cheeks and at last her lips. He never wanted to let her go.

And he refused to think about the moment when he'd be forced to do just that.

~

Jane had experienced a great deal of sex and yet what she shared with Ripley was entirely unique. It was, of course, what she'd feared from the first moment they met, when the connection had felt so raw and powerful. Friendship had pushed it aside—she'd ignored it rather than fallen into it.

But when his body was joined with hers? When their panting breaths merged and their sweat mingled? In those moments she knew that he felt different because he *was*. He was more. He was everything.

He lifted his head from her shoulder and smiled at her. "I'm famished."

She laughed. "I would assume so. You worked up quite the appetite."

He dropped his lips to hers and the kiss was gentle and brief. "Why don't we go down for the famous supper spread Mr. Fergus couldn't stop talking about?"

She stared up into his face in surprise. So often her interactions with men had been in secret. There were places where women like her belonged and it was rarely at a man's table. Even a protector's. So even though Ripley had pretended she was his wife, somehow she had expected he might put up that same wall between what was proper and what wasn't.

"Are you in there, Jane?" he asked, his brow wrinkling. "Have I pleasured you to the loss of reason?"

"You are quite full of yourself, aren't you? No, I have reason, just found myself woolgathering. I'd love to share supper."

"Good." He got up and quickly tucked himself back into place. It took him all of two minutes to look ready to go.

"I think it will take me a bit longer," she said, rising and stretching muscles sore from pleasurable use.

"Then let me help." He swept up her gown from where she'd discarded it on the floor and shook it out. She smoothed her wrinkled chemise and then gripped his forearm as she balanced herself to step in.

He was gentle as he helped her dress. Fastened the buttons he'd watched her strip for him earlier. When he touched her, it wasn't meant to seduce, even though even the grazing glances did just that. This man drove her wild, that was all there was to it.

But at last she was dressed and she moved to sit at the dressing table. She laughed at her cock-eyed hair, messy from his fingers. "This won't do. I think I lost some pins. Will you look for them?"

He gave her a mock salute and did that as she used her fingers to comb out the locks since she didn't want to find her brush in the portmanteau she hadn't bothered to open once they'd entered the room. He brought her a handful and watched as she swept her hair up in a loose bun at the nape of her neck.

"You're very good at that."

She smiled at him in the reflection of the mirror. "It comes with the trade, I think. A woman like me has to know how to fix herself with speed and efficiency."

"I suppose that's true. It certainly gives you advantage over ladies who need so much help."

She laughed. "You should have seen Esme when she first left her old life. She was useless with gowns and brushes. I had to teach her how to take care of herself."

"You did a fine job," he said softly. The compliment warmed her more than it should.

"So did you."

They stared at each other in the reflection for a moment. Until it became a little uncomfortable for Jane because it was far too close. She got up and faced him with a false smile. "I'm ready now."

"Very good."

He took her arm like he truly was her husband and together they went down to the dining hall where others were already seated. Staff brought out wine and food that smelled so good Jane's stomach growled. It was all Scottish fare, probably because of the owner's heritage, and she practically bounced at the idea of finely fried fish and potatoes.

Mr. Fergus waved to them after they were seated and Ripley returned the wave. He pushed back from the place he'd just taken and said, "I want to discuss something with the man. Give me a moment."

She nodded and watched him as he crossed the room. She'd always loved to watch him move through a crowd. Ripley carried himself like a warrior, no matter how long it had been since he fought in a ring. He had a command of the room that everyone bowed to and people moved in his wake. Plus, now that she knew the exact arrangements of the glorious muscles beneath his clothes, she enjoyed watching them ripple all the more.

The two men talked for a moment and Fergus looked at her for a brief moment before he nodded and rushed away to do whatever Ripley had asked when it came to their horses or accommodations.

Ripley returned and settled into his place, draping his napkin across his lap. "He seems a decent fellow, even if he talks ceaselessly."

"I suppose he's in the right business for it," Jane said with a laugh. "It's always a trick to know when to speak and when to be silent when one is serving the needs of others."

Before Ripley could answer a very pretty lady with dark hair and a round face with a wide smile approached them. "Oh, good evening Mr. and Mrs. Ripley," she said.

Jane was startled by being called his wife again, even if she'd known it would happen. She kept her gaze away from Ripley's so she wouldn't see his reaction.

"Good evening," he said in return.

"I'm Mrs. Fergus. I hope your finding your accommodations well?"

Now Jane did look at her. She had the same friendliness that her husband did and a bright joy that seemed to warm the room. "Very much."

"I'm pleased to hear it. May I tell you what we've got on hand for the meal?"

"The fish smells divine," Jane said. "I cannot think of having anything else."

Mrs. Fergus's expression lit up. "Very good. It's also my favorite."

"And I'll do the same," Ripley said.

"I'll bring you ale in the interim." The woman swept away.

"Would you like wine instead?" Ripley asked. "Or something stronger?"

"No, ale is fine," she replied with a smile. "Always the gentlemen."

"Never once," he teased back.

But she knew better. Ripley was rough, but he was always the best of what she considered gentlemanly. It made him so hard to resist. That and a great deal else. She reached out to touch his hand and he spread his fingers so that hers interlocked with his.

At that moment, Mrs. Fergus returned and placed two mugs

before them. "Ah, young love. I do adore seeing it. How long have you two been married?"

Jane stiffened at the idea she would have to concoct a backstory with the man before her. But Ripley seemed to have none of that hesitation. He held Jane's stare evenly as he said, "I knew I was hers years ago. She marked me from the start."

Jane's mouth dropped open a bit and she couldn't ignore the flutter her heart gave at that response and the intense look he gave her when he said it. Mrs. Fergus cooed with pleasure. "I do love a romantic tale. Let me know if you need anything before the food comes."

When Mrs. Fergus left them, Jane slid her hand from his. "You're laying it on a bit thick, aren't you?"

He shook his head. "I'm telling the truth."

"What?" She wrinkled her brow. "You said I marked you. How in the world could that be the truth?"

He hesitated a moment and then he lifted his hand and slid his fingertip across the harsh white mark of the scar through his eyebrow. Her hands began to shake and she shoved them under the table to steady them on her knees.

"Explain," she managed to squeak out. "Please. Because I couldn't be the cause of the famous scar."

CHAPTER 11

Ripley hadn't intended to tell Jane about her role in the scar. The story revealed too much, and she was too clever not to understand just that. But the longer he spent with her, the more he entangled himself physically and emotionally in her life, the harder it was to contain the feelings that burned in him. And now that had caused this burst of honesty that made her eyes wide and almost fearful.

He cleared his throat. "You attended a fight of mine years ago. With Beast MacDougal."

She blinked and he realized she didn't recall it. Of course, that made sense. It wasn't a pivotal moment of her life, it had just been another night out with some prick who used her.

"I-I do remember seeing you fight before we met," she said slowly. Carefully, it seemed. As if she didn't want to stumble into some trap he was laying for her. "I don't know the other man's name."

"Did I bleed?" he asked.

She nodded. "He caught you with a hard punch and you did bleed. But you already had the scar by then, didn't you? You were always known for the scar."

She looked at it then and he reached up to trace it again out of habit. "No. I was distracted from the fight. He hit me just right to split my eyebrow. And this lovely mark is the result."

At that moment, Mrs. Fergus returned with plates of fish and fried potato. She was talking and smiling and Jane did an admirable job of interacting even though her gaze kept flitting to his.

"I'll stop by the table later to check in on you," Mrs. Fergus said. "Oh, and Mr. Ripley, they've begun filling the tub in your chamber. It will be ready by the time you finish eating."

She smiled and walked away. Jane stared at him full-on now. She didn't touch her food. "What were you distracted by?" she asked as if they hadn't been interrupted in their earlier conversation.

He reached for her hand again. "You." Her nostrils flared and he continued, "We pivoted while grappling and something in the crowd caught my eye. The most beautiful woman I'd ever seen. I lost concentration for a moment and MacDougal was a wily one and caught me."

To his surprise, her face crumpled. "I-I was the reason you were scarred."

"It was my distraction and my fault," he said. "And I rather like the scar. As you said, it's become one of my distinguishing characteristics."

She bent her head and focused on her food. She picked up her fork, but she only traced it over the fish and potatoes she'd been so excited to try only a few moments before. "Ripley," she whispered.

He shrugged. "This can't be a surprise, Jane. We don't come from worlds where we mince our words, do we? It was obvious from the start that we were attracted to each other. You wanted me and I wanted you. There's no shame in that."

"Perhaps not," she said. "But *you* are respectable now. You own a thriving club that men of power and rank trip over their own feet to join because it's as important as their membership at White's or the Donville Masquerade. You've built yourself a life. And I'm...I'm still...me."

He hated how she diminished herself. She was as scarred as he was, just inside. "Don't elevate me. We both made our living on our backs."

"It isn't the same. You know it. A boxer could be respected, as you were when you fought and are now." She shook her head. "The woman you saw in my shop, the viscountess who called me out for what I was, she was only the first. She won't be the last. I scarred you once, but I care too much to scar you again."

He caught his breath. "Jane—"

"Don't," she whispered, and tears sparkled in her eyes. She blinked at them, pushing them away just as he knew she'd been pushing them away all her life. "We'll go to Copperworth. We'll find my sister and then...then I think we need to stay away from each other."

Ripley had experienced pain in his life. Broken bones, deep bruises. Once an opponent had tried to stab his heart and Ripley had caught the blade in his hand, slashing his palm deeply. But none of that hurt as much as Jane's words, at the idea that she'd rather run from the connection that was so plain than risk what it could change.

But he'd always known that was the potential price of finally giving in to what he wanted. She would push if he pulled, just as she had any other time they'd even come close to this. She would run. Her life would make any other reaction difficult for her. And he'd have to honor her request. Honor her rejection even if it destroyed some vital part of him.

She shook her head at his silence. "I'm poison, Ripley."

He wanted to scream at those words, but instead he took her hand. "I don't think that's your voice saying that."

She sucked in a harsh breath. "I assume you mean it's my mother. She'd know best, wouldn't she? I'm just like her." Before he could argue, she tugged her hand from his and stood. "I'm tired. I think I'll go up, take that bath you've so kindly arranged. We've a long day tomorrow."

If pulling away was in her nature, to fight was in his. He wanted to rise with her, argue with her in the middle of the dining hall, kiss her until she couldn't pretend that this thing between them was anything but good.

And yet he did none of that. If he loved her, which he did, he needed to be more careful than a bull rushing through glass without thought. He'd learned to be strategic as a fighter. He would be strategic in this, as well.

"I understand," he said softly.

She seemed surprised he would respect her request, but she nodded and then slipped away through the room. He watched her every step, his heart breaking. And he had no idea what to do next to prevent her from walking away from him for good.

Jane sat in the warm, fragrant waters of the tub, staring up at the ceiling. The sensations were lovely, but she couldn't relax. Not when Ripley's words echoed in her head. How he was hers since the first moment he'd seen her. How he was marked by her. He didn't seem to care that the mark was in the form of a scar caused by injury. A permanent reminder of the damage she could cause.

She loved him. That had always been a fact she ignored, pushed away, pretended wasn't real. Just as she'd pretended she didn't know he loved her in return. Now it was impossible to ignore those facts. They were too close to turn away from. And they were problems she had to deal with because knowing they loved each other didn't change what she'd said to him at supper. Everyone she'd ever loved, she'd hurt. Everyone who'd ever loved her had come to despise her.

She couldn't bear it if he joined that small, terrible club.

"I'll leave London." She started because she hadn't meant to say those words out loud. But they gave her strength and she sat up a bit straighter. "I'll take Nora, because we *must* find Nora, and go to the country. I'll start over. It will be better for Esme so she won't try to continue being a friend to someone so far from herself. It will be better for Nora so she can be away from whatever happened to her. It will be better for…for Ripley."

Hearing the words out loud, the falter in her voice when she said the last sentence, it made her sick. But it was right. She was right.

She heard the door open behind the privacy screen that protected the bath from the larger room and stiffened.

"It's me," Ripley said, his voice soft.

She heard him shift, heard the door close. His footfalls came across the room, certain and unwavering. She could see him move in her mind, an easy image after years of observation.

But he didn't come around to look at her. Instead she heard him doing something in the larger room.

She cleared her throat. "It was kind to call out that it was you."

"Well, I'd never want to frighten you." There was a slight hesitation and then he added, "Or hurt you."

She sighed. "I know. It's the same for me."

"May I come around?"

This man who had seen her naked, licked every inch of her body, asked her permission. No wonder she loved him, he was unlike anyone she'd ever encountered.

"Yes," she whispered. How could she refuse, even if she already knew how this would end, that she would leave his life and eventually he would see the value in her being gone. But it wasn't over yet, was it? Wasn't there some way to hold it separate from the inevitable?

He came around the screen. He was so impossibly tall, even more so from her angle below him in the tub. And he was beautiful. She stared at his face in the firelight, memorizing all the angles of him, all the marks from his violent past, all the little expressions that made him the man he was.

"I want you to know that I'll do whatever you like, Jane. I told you that before. You never have to tie my hands."

She understood what he meant and her heart swelled with even more of the love which felt so powerful now that she could no longer deny it.

His breath was shaky as he added, "But I'd like to have this time with you. Please."

She gripped the edge of the tub at the "please". It seemed they both wanted the same thing, as was often true. She knew what the loss would feel like, she wanted the moments they had left.

Slowly she stood up, water dripping down her body like a waterfall. She knew exactly what she looked like and how he would react was equally easy to guess. His pupils dilated, he licked his lips like he was looking at a feast and he was starving.

He held out a hand and she took it, steadying herself as she stepped from the tub. Then he pulled her forward and flattened her wet body against his chest. He didn't seem to care that she was soaking him as he bent his head and claimed her mouth.

For that moment she was his. And she forced herself to forget everything else as he gathered her up and carried her to the bed where he would claim her over and over for the rest of the night.

CHAPTER 12

In truth, Ripley hadn't expected Jane to discuss their painful conversation. It wasn't in her nature to do so, and since she was already drowning in so many fears and responsibilities over her sister, he hadn't pushed.

So they'd made love and eaten the food he'd brought up for her and then done it all again. It was as if what had been said at supper never happened.

And now he observed her across the carriage seat, watching her worry her hands in her lap as she stared out the window like she could find her sister faster if she caught the first glimpse of the seminary where Nora had been last seen. She hadn't looked at him for the past three-quarters of an hour. She was putting up walls, balling up her pain in a place he couldn't reach. It broke his heart.

"There it is," she breathed.

He leaned forward to look. There was a big manor rising in the distance. It was impressive, that was for certain, with gabled windows and spires.

"I'll want to speak to Miss Knightly, the headmistress," she said. "The awful woman who wrote me the letter about Nora being missing."

The color was gone from her cheeks and he took her hand. She glanced at him. "I'll be there," he said.

She worried her lip and he was brought back to a moment the previous night when he'd done the same, nipping her there while she rippled around his cock in orgasm.

"May I...would you mind if I repeat the lie you told the innkeeper yesterday?"

He swallowed hard. "You mean that you're my wife?"

She nodded. "Miss Knightly may not know exactly what I am... *was*. She never would have allowed my sister to attend her seminary if she had, but she's always judged me regardless. She might be easier if she sees me in the respectability of a marriage."

He tried not to let his heart race at the idea of her as his wife, just as he'd struggled to do the previous day, and merely said, "I understand. Mrs. Ripley you'll be and I'll do all I can to smooth the interaction."

"Thank you," she gasped out, her relief obvious. Her hand fluttered as if she wished to take his, but she kept it in her lap and they were silent as the carriage stopped on the large circular drive before the school. He stepped out first and guided her from the carriage. She stared up into his face and she was so pale that all he wanted to do was sweep her up and rush her off to safety.

Only he couldn't. So he merely tucked her hand into the crook of his elbow and said, "We *will* find her, Jane."

And he hoped that promise wouldn't be another lie that would break her heart and soul.

Jane picked at a loose thread on her sleeve as she and Ripley sat in a small parlor where they'd been placed after asking to see Miss Knightly. She could hear the soft voices of young women talking and giggling in the hallways. She could see more of them outside on the grounds. She shook her head. Would she even recognize Nora if she saw her out there? After all, she hadn't seen her sister for years. She wasn't a little girl anymore.

The door to the parlor opened and Miss Knightly entered the room. She was a tall woman with sleek black hair pulled back tightly in a bun. She had a severe face, all hard angles and lines that commanded respect.

"I was not expecting you," the woman said with no preamble as Jane staggered to her feet. Ripley did the same, though with much more ease. "It is a breach of good manners, Miss Kendall."

Jane felt herself shrink a little. The unspoken implication was that Miss Knightly had expected no less from a person such as her.

Before she could formulate some kind of response, Ripley stepped forward. "She is Mrs. Ripley now. And you must be Miss Knightly." He extended his hand. "I've heard so much about you."

The woman seemed flummoxed as she looked Ripley up and down. "I…er, I hadn't realized you had married. My felicitations."

"Yes," Ripley said, and placed a light hand on Jane's waist. "It's very new."

Miss Knightly cleared her throat, giving Ripley one more glance before she focused those sharp eyes back on Jane. "I imagine you are here regarding your sister."

"Yes," Jane managed, and tried to put herself back together. "There has still been no sign of Nora since she left your care. Your letter gave me so few answers, I must understand what happened. What the circumstances were of her departure."

Miss Knightly's lips pursed. "And I gave you all the particulars I knew in the letter. It cannot be a surprise to you that Honora has done something so wild. I sent you the various reports of her behavior over the last year. Not every young woman wishes to be respectable, Miss…Mrs. Ripley."

Jane stiffened her spine. "My sister attended your school without incident for the better part of a decade. It was only in the last year that she changed. Did that not trouble you? Did you not question the reasons rather than merely judge her for them?"

Miss Knightly huffed out a breath. "You've wasted your time coming here, Mrs. Ripley. I've nothing else of value to share."

Jane gripped her hands at her sides, but before she could scream or lash out or burst into tears, none of which would help, Ripley stepped forward.

"Now then, Miss Knightly, surely you must understand my wife's concern. She knows what a fine job your institution has done with Honora. We only wish to uncover where she might have gone so that we might collect her and return her to her loving family."

"The family that did not allow her home during holidays?" Miss Knightly snapped.

Jane turned her head. No, she hadn't let Honora home over the years. Where could she have sent her? Back to their mother and her abuse? To Jane's home where what she did and was would have been increasingly clear to an impressionable girl?

Ripley's jaw set. She could see the shift in him from his initial attempts to soothe this woman to more intense anger at her responses. "I would not question Jane's love for her sister if I were you, Miss Knightly."

The headmistress looked at him, was intelligent enough to see the warning through his quiet admonishment, and she swallowed. "Of course not."

Jane drew in a short breath and tried again. "And understand I'm not questioning your seminary, either. Over the years I could see the good influence you had on Nora. Perhaps I did fail in my duties to her, but I don't want to do that now, not when it could be a matter of life or death. Please, please won't you consider what you might know, even something that seems unimportant?"

Miss Knightly put her hands on her hips. "Is there an issue of understanding, Mrs. Ripley? There is nothing I can tell you."

Jane turned her head and bit back a roar of pain and frustration.

Ripley reached for her and took her hand, squeezing gently. In that moment she saw the question in his stare. She understood, without him having to say a word, that he was requesting her permission to unleash a dragon, since something softer and more proper hadn't given them results. She hesitated briefly and then nodded.

The change in him was immediate. His gaze darkened, his shoulders came back a fraction and he turned to Miss Knightly with a focused stare.

"I'm a very good judge of character, Miss Knightly," he said, his voice still dangerously soft. "I can read people—it's a special gift I developed in a life a person like you would easily dismiss. I noticed you said you couldn't tell my wife more, not that you didn't know more. A slip, something minor in theory, but I think words having meaning. I can tell you know more about what happened to Jane's sister."

"I—" Miss Knightly's eyes widened. "No."

His nostrils flared ever so slightly, but Jane still looked for smoke to curl from them. Fire. "Let me explain to you what will happen next. You will tell us *everything* you know about Nora's disappearance and turn over any evidence you have about where she's gone. You'll also grant us access to speak to Nora's friends."

"I'm telling you I know nothing." Miss Knightly folded her arms, but she looked less certain. "And I cannot just allow you to speak to anyone you wish to."

Ripley continued as if hadn't spoken at all. "If you don't do this, then I'll have no choice but to post a notice about her going missing into every paper in this country. And I'll be certain to include the fact that she disappeared from this establishment under *your* care."

Jane jerked her gaze to him and then back to Miss Knightly. The headmistress's cheeks had gone pale. It seemed Ripley had hit upon a consequence that actually mattered.

"You can sit up there on that high horse, but what you do is perform a service." Ripley arched a brow. "And people like you live and die on your reputation. I doubt you want the entire country to know it isn't safe to send their daughters to you because you'd be so careless as to lose them. Do we understand each other better now?"

Miss Knightly opened and shut her mouth and she looked at Jane, but this time it seemed she was seeking assistance. Jane stepped up closer to Ripley and slid a hand through his elbow. He reached his other hand across and covered hers and it was like he pulled away some of the weight of her fear. They faced this woman as a united front and Jane was utterly aware of the moment Miss Knightly realized she was not facing off with individuals without power.

The headmistress let out a long, shaky sigh. "We understand each other perfectly, Mr. Ripley. Of course you and your wife have concerns about Honora. I'll...I truly *don't* have much information."

Ripley's expression was softer now that he'd won. Jane was fascinated by that. He only pushed to the point that he needed to. He didn't use power as a cudgel. But then again, that was how he'd fought in the ring, as well. She remembered so many fights when he'd backed off the moment his opponent was stunned, even when the crowd demanded more violence and blood.

"We'll be grateful to have all you know," he said.

"While Honora's behavior did become more difficult in the last year, the past few months were different," Miss Knightly said slowly. "She was disciplined more than once for skipping classes or being found absent from her dormitory at night."

Jane gasped. "You wrote to me about some poor behavior, but never that she was missing like that."

Ripley squeezed her hand gently and she looked up at him. She saw his gentle understanding, his support, but she also saw that he was trying to rein her in. He was the one who wasn't emotional about this situation. She dropped her head.

"Please continue," she whispered.

Miss Knightly shifted. "I have some of her things that were left behind. I intended to send them on to you when I had the time. But that's truly all I know."

Jane pulled away from Ripley and paced over to the window. She could hardly breathe as the facts hit her from all sides. This was no information at all, unless somehow her sister had left clues of what had happened to her in her things. And why would she do that? Nora was no fool, she had always been clever. If she'd left of her own volition, she wouldn't have wanted anyone to find her. And if she hadn't...well, how would she have known to leave breadcrumbs for a sister desperate to find her?

So this trip, just like the one to see her mother, was a waste of time. They were no closer to finding her sister and now she had no idea of what to do next.

She heard Ripley speaking softly to Miss Knightly, but she couldn't hear the words. She continued to stare out into the garden behind the school, watching as girls strolled by in pairs. Every time she saw one with dark blonde hair like her sister, she caught her breath.

"Oh, Nora, where are you?" she whispered.

She heard the door behind her close and pivoted. Miss Knightly had departed and Ripley was coming toward her in a few long strides. She stepped into his arms without hesitation and he held her tightly, as if he could somehow save her with just his warmth and presence.

He almost could.

She looked up at him at last. "I've wasted so much of your time and money."

He shook his head. "You haven't done either of those things. We know now that she was restless and unhappy and that something changed in the last few months of her being here. That leans toward her leaving the school of her own volition. And that's better than her being taken, isn't it? Miss Knightly said she would bring the items Nora left behind and also have Nora's two best mates join us shortly to discuss the matter further."

Jane pulled away from his arms and let out her breath in a shaky sigh. "Thank you for managing this. I would never have convinced her to do anything at all for me."

"That's why I'm here," he said. "To support you however you need me to do so."

She smiled despite the situation. "When you were facing off with her I kept thinking of how you were in the ring. You were treating her like a fighter."

His lips tightened. "Well, I certainly didn't intend to take the confrontation to violence."

She shook her head. "Oh no, I didn't mean that. I meant that when you fought, you fought with your mind. You were always thinking, I could see it back then. It was always such a beautiful thing to watch you. And you used those same tools today. I never would have thought to threaten her with blows to her school's reputation."

"You see me through rose glass," he said with a smile. "Just because of a few orgasms."

"More than a few," she teased back gently.

He shrugged. "I suppose that to threaten to reveal the lack of care toward her charges was the best strategy under these circumstances."

"You see," Jane said. "Always thinking. Do you...do you miss fighting?"

He swallowed. "I assume you're asking me this to pass the time until we can question Nora's friends?"

She nodded. "It helps to think of something else. But also, I'm curious. I've watched you fight, I've seen you train others, but we've never talked much about it, and it was and is such a big part of who you are."

He shifted, and in that moment she realized that this was an uncomfortable topic for him. Despite the fact that he'd been a champion, that he was the best at what he'd done and that he continued to make his living from his skills, he found no pleasure in discussing it.

"You don't have to tell me," she said softly.

"You've cut yourself open for me. I suppose it is an even trade." He let out a shaky sigh. "I originally fought because I had to. I didn't want my mother to have to do what she did. Some of her protectors were fine enough and treated her with some level of respect. But others weren't. I wanted to…to save her."

Jane caught her breath. How often had she thought the same of her mother, especially when she was younger. In her case she thought if she could save her, her mother would be better.

"I turned to fighting to make money eventually. Found I was good at violence." He shook his head. "You speak of my days in the ring as if they were something to be proud of. But I hurt people for money."

"No," she said. "I suppose sometimes that was the outcome. But don't forget that I watched you, Cam."

They both froze as she realized she had called him by that short-ened version of his first name. The one she only used when they were intimately entangled. But then again, this conversation *felt* intimate when it was all about pain and regret. About a self-judge-ment she wanted to ease.

"I watched you, *Cam*," she repeated so he'd know it wasn't some-thing she apologized for. "I saw what you did in when you fought. You never went further than the fight required. Your opponents stepped into the ring with as much information as you did. They knew the risk as much as you did. But you were one of the few champions who never killed an opponent. That was because you weren't doing it to hurt others."

He rubbed a hand over his face. "No, I suppose that was never my goal."

"I know it wasn't. Do you know why people loved to watch you? Why those who came to see you still remember you and pay for your drinks?"

"Why?"

"Because there was poetry to you in the ring," she said, and stepped toward him. She didn't touch him, but looked up into his eyes, holding him steady just as he'd been holding her steady since her sister's disappearance. "It was like dance with you. A graceful control of every muscle, every fiber of your being. An almost preternatural focus on your opponent." She did reach up now and traced the scar she'd been part of creating. "Well, most of the time."

He caught her hand and pressed a kiss to her palm. "I think you credit me too much."

"And you credit yourself too little. So perhaps the truth lies somewhere in between."

The door to the parlor opened and Ripley released her as they faced Miss Knightly's return as a unit. She held a small box in her hands.

"This is all there is left," she said, and handed it over to Ripley.

Jane stared. "That's all? No clothing, nothing else of value?"

"It appears she took it all with her," Miss Knightly said. "Now I have Miss Fairfax and Miss Greenwich to speak to you. I'll send them in."

She pivoted and left the room. Jane gripped the box with all her might. "There's so little."

"And that's another mark in the column that Nora left on her own volition," Ripley said.

"I suppose that's true," Jane whispered, and tried to be cheered by that fact. It was the better of the possible scenarios.

She straightened as two young women came through the door to the study. They were both about the same height as she was. Both were very pretty, one all curves, the other willowy. They were women, not girls. And that meant her sister was a woman, too. It was so hard to picture her that way and not as the child Jane had wept over when she left her at the school, knowing she would hardly see her again in order to protect her.

But she hadn't protected her in the end, had she?

Miss Knightly followed them in. "This is Miss Fairfax," she said, indicating the willowy girl with darker hair. "And Miss Greenwich."

"Thank you, Miss Knightly," Ripley said, moving to all but herd her from the room. "We won't be long."

"I think that—" Miss Knightly began, but he closed the door in her face.

Jane was grateful for it. She knew the girls would be less likely to speak in front of the headmistress if they thought they would get in trouble. She drew a long breath and then stepped toward them with what she hoped was a friendly smile rather than a desperate expression. She noted Ripley stood back, allowing her to handle them.

Once again, he was reading the situation, just as she'd complimented him for doing in the ring.

"Good afternoon, thank you both so much for agreeing to speak to me."

The girls exchanged a quick glance and Miss Greenwich was the one who spoke. "You're Nora's sister, yes? That's what Miss Knightly said."

"I am," Jane said. "And I know you two are her friends. So we all deeply care for her."

Miss Fairfax pursed her lips a little, as if she didn't entirely agree with that assessment, but she didn't say anything about it. But the expression stung. It seemed Nora had spoken to her friends about Jane, and not in a positive light. She'd have to tread carefully.

"Nora is missing," Jane said. "I think you both know that she disappeared from the school. I only want to know where she's gone. If she's safe."

Miss Greenwich looked her up and down with the judgmental look only a young woman of a certain age could perfect. "She talked about you, you know. I don't know why you'd pretend to care about her when you didn't even see her all this time."

Jane turned her head because the words hit like a slap. Ripley moved like he'd come forward, but she held up a hand. "I realize Nora was angry with me. She had every right to be. There were reasons I had to keep her from me and from our mother. I was trying to protect her and perhaps I didn't do it well. I hurt her in the process, that's clear now."

How the truth of those words stung, reminding her of what her nature was. When she did find Nora, they would have a great deal to discuss, it seemed.

"We can save all of us a great deal of time," Miss Fairfax said. "Neither of us knows anything about where Nora is or why she disappeared. Isn't that right, Gertie?"

The other young woman dropped her gaze. "Yes. That's right."

Jane didn't believe them. How could she when one of them wouldn't stop looking at the floor and the other was holding such intense eye contact that it felt like an over correction? She shook her head. "Please. Whatever you think of me, know that I only want to be certain my sister isn't in danger. Even if she ran away on her own, that doesn't mean she isn't in trouble."

Miss Fairfax folded her arms. There was a steel in her stare, protective and unyielding. Jane wouldn't get through to her—she'd already made up her mind about the situation and nothing that was said would likely break through that shell. But the other girl, Gertie, was shifting.

So Jane focused her attention on her. "Please," she said more softly. "If you haven't heard from her since she vanished, you must be concerned, even if you believe she left of her own accord. If she's happy, I won't bother her." Not entirely true, perhaps, depending on the circumstances, but at this point honesty wasn't the best policy. "Please, Miss Greenwich."

The young woman lifted her gaze, but before she could say anything, Miss Fairfax caught her arm and tugged her closer. "We don't know anything. There's nothing else to say. Come, Gertie. We're meant to be in lessons."

She tugged the other girl toward the door.

"Oh no, please wait!" Jane cried out, rushing toward them, but they were already bolting down the hall and Miss Knightly stepped in the way. She had clearly gathered herself and she appeared stern and unyielding again.

"It seems the young women are finished discussing whatever it is you wished to talk about, Mrs. Ripley. There's nothing else to do or say. I'll have your carriage brought back around. You can wait on the drive."

Jane looked back over her shoulder at Ripley and he met her stare evenly. There was such comfort in that stare, such certainty that she couldn't feel in this moment when it seemed like the floor had dropped out beneath her feet and all she could do was fall hopelessly.

He nodded at her slightly before he came to her and took her arm. Silently they walked to the foyer together and out onto the drive. Miss Knightly said a curt farewell that Jane hardly heard, and then she left them to wait.

"So much for her bloody manners," Ripley muttered.

"She never knew what I was," Jane said softly. "But she sensed I wasn't worthy of manners, I suppose. As did those girls. They knew more, but they didn't think I'd earned it."

Ripley wrapped his arm around her. "We did find something out, though. Their lack of concern with Nora's whereabouts, that says to me that they knew she intended to go. She ran, Jane. She wasn't taken against her will."

She nodded. "I suppose that's something. Even though I know full well that just because she left with some grand future in mind doesn't mean that's what she walked into."

Ripley drew a breath as if to respond, but before he could there was a tap on Jane's shoulder. She swung around to find Miss Greenwich standing there. She glanced over her shoulder toward the house and then handed over a little folded message.

"What is this?" Jane said as she took it.

"That's all I can do," Miss Greenwich responded, and then bolted back inside.

Jane glanced up at Ripley. The carriage was arriving now, but she ignored it as she unfolded the note. The hand was sloppy and shaky, on a scrap piece of paper that had class notes written on the back. It read:

There was a young man. I don't know his name, but Nora was going to elope.

CHAPTER 13

Ripley couldn't see what the note Jane had been handed said, but he knew it wasn't positive by the way she wobbled on her feet. He caught her elbow, steadying her before he opened the carriage door.

"Come, Janie," he said softly as he helped her into the vehicle. She slumped against the carriage wall, the note crumpled in her hand. He looked up at the drive with a frown. "Just take us somewhere close and stop. I'll give you further direction after."

The man inclined his head and Ripley joined Jane in the carriage. She was trembling, but not crying. Somehow he wished she were. That she could release some of those fears and heartbreaks that lined every part of her face.

He reached out and cupped her hand, smoothing his fingers over hers before he slipped the note from her hand and read it. He glanced up. "So she's eloped with some young man. Jane, this could be the best scenario."

She shook her head. "You're trying to appease me. To calm me, but how can I be calm? My sister has run off with God knows who. The kind of man who would do something so—"

"Potentially romantic," Ripley interrupted gently.

Jane rolled her eyes as if the concept didn't exist for her. "Ugh."

He had set the box Miss Knightly had given to them onto the seat beside him when he joined her and now he motioned to her. "Why don't we look through this? There may be more information that could help us find her."

Jane nodded and he handed it over. She balanced the small item on her lap and tugged it open. They looked inside together. There were a few more letters and a ring. She drew it out with a shake of her head.

"I bought this for her years ago," she whispered. "She truly despises me."

"She's of an age to lash out," he said. "When we find her, you'll repair the relationship. You'll atone for your mistakes and eventually she will, too."

"You are so certain she could love me again?" Jane asked.

He nodded. "Because you're impossible not to love."

Her expression softened, even as her gaze darted from his. He was revealing too much. He didn't care in that moment. In the end, it would all come out anyway. There was no way he ended this battle without another scar. The first one had been worth it, he could only hope this one would be too.

"What are the letters?" he asked as she slipped her sister's ring onto her pinky finger.

She drew them out, looking them over, unfolding them to read. "Seems to mostly be letters from friends over the years. Dates are around holidays when she remained at the school." He could see her regrets on her face when she added, "I should have explained better why she couldn't be with me or our mother during those times. Christ, I was a fool."

"You did the best you could," he said.

She lifted her gaze. "But it wasn't what she needed. It hurt her."

"And you'll accept that responsibility."

"You make it sound so easy," she whispered, bending her head.

He flipped over the next letter in the pile and stopped as he unfolded it. An iciness settled over him as he scanned the words. Then it was replaced by anger. He lifted his gaze to Jane, still staring at her hands.

"Jane," he said gently. He was about to hurt her, he hated that. "Jane, this letter is from your mother."

Just as he expected, the reaction was swift and powerful. She lunged forward to the edge of the carriage seat and snatched the letter from his hands. "What?" She almost tore the cheap pages as she read them once, twice. Then she looked up. "She lied. My mother lied to me that she hadn't been in contact with Nora."

"Yes," he said softly. "I couldn't see that, I'm sorry."

"She's expert at manipulation, it isn't your fault. But *I* should have known." She squeezed her eyes shut briefly and then read some of the letter to him in a shaky tone, "*If this Hugo wants you, you should do all you can to secure him, Nora. Grandsons of titled men don't fall out of trees for women like us. You could help me and if you do that I'll be more willing to meet with you.*"

Ripley lifted a hand to his mouth as nausea rolled through him. Jane's cheeks had gone pale and the two of them stared at each other as the ramifications of her mother's words sat heavy in the air.

"How could she encourage my sister in this way, manipulate her with affection? And how could she lie to me about her? Lie about being in contact, lie about knowing anything," Jane whispered. "She's a monster, entirely self-concerned."

"She is," Ripley agreed. "And *that* is why you're nothing like her, Jane." He slipped the letter from her hands. "Whatever she said to you for all those years, it's just as much a manipulation and a lie as whatever she told Nora." He glanced over the letter. "We have a name now. Hugo isn't a particularly common first name, I don't think. And we know he's the grandson of a someone of rank."

"Which gets me exactly nowhere. That viscount's wife was an exception, not a rule. I was a courtesan for mostly middle-class people, Ripley. I don't know titled types."

"But Esme and Delacourt do," he said.

Her lips tightened and her eyes slid shut. "I was hoping not to drag them into my mess."

He caught her hands and she lifted those beautiful blue eyes to his. Eyes that were filled with so much pain now that it crushed him down to his soul to see it. And to know that there wasn't much he could do to help anymore except support her. Hold her up if she needed it.

"People who love you *want* to help, Jane." She dropped her gaze to her lap again, but she nodded and that was enough for now. He continued, "We'll go back to London. Discuss this with them, try to determine our next steps. Together, Jane."

She looked up at him and then she slowly traced the line of his jaw with her fingertips. She let out a low, shaky sigh. "I won't turn down the help. I couldn't now. I already owe you far more than I could ever repay. By the time this is done I fear you'll regret it and me."

He wanted to argue that with her. To patch together all these places that turned out to be broken beneath her hard façade. But this wasn't the time. So instead he shifted over to her side of the carriage, tucked her into his side, and simply held her.

~

The inn on the way to London that they stopped at far into the night wasn't as fancy as the others where they'd stayed during their travels. But it had food and beds, which was all Jane needed.

Of course, she wasn't using either as she sat before the fire, an untouched plate at her side, staring into the flames. All she could think about was Nora and all her fears for what was happening to her.

All she could think about was her failings and the failings of their mother and the world at large.

There was a light knock on the door and Jane started before she called out, "Come in."

It was Ripley, of course. He entered the chamber and shut the door. His gaze flitted to the plate still untouched by her side. "You haven't eaten."

She shook her head. "I couldn't."

"Janie, starving yourself will only make you less able to concentrate," he insisted. "You must be sharp for what will come next."

She gave him a look. He was saying whatever he felt would force her to eat. And it was working. She pulled the plate closer and speared one of the roasted potatoes. As she chewed, she shook her head. "You are far too good at knowing what I need to hear."

He took a seat across from hers and gave her a weak smile. "I'm good at knowing what you need. And you're too clever not to recognize I'm right."

For a while she ate and he only sat with her in silence. There was something comforting about that. His calm made her calmer, somehow. His presence kept her warm in the chill of her fears.

At last, though, she set aside her plate half-eaten and settled back in her chair with a long sigh. It was only then that he spoke again, "Tell me."

She pinched her lips together. "Haven't I dumped out my troubles enough? God, I have swept into your life and turned it upside down. In the end, you'll despise me."

"Not possible." His voice was low and rough. He sat on the edge of his chair, draping his elbows over his knees. His focus on her was so intent that it felt like she was being speared into place. *Tell me.*

Her breath came shorter and harsher at that order. Her life had been spent hiding her feelings. They'd never been safe with her mother, she'd feared hurting her sister. In her life as a lightskirt and mistress, she'd been nothing but a doll to play with for the lovers who met her. They didn't want her emotions, just her body. Even with Esme, who she considered herself closest to, she kept much of herself secret. Why hurt her?

But with Ripley? He made it impossible to hide. It was as if he had keys to her heart, to her soul, and he could open her up any time he liked. That was the danger of love, wasn't it? That was why she'd avoided the attraction that had always sparked between them. She feared *this*. Being not just perceived, but seen. Understood. A person who could do that held a great deal of power.

And yet abuse of power wasn't what terrified her. It was opening doors that she knew might not ever fully close again.

"I'm…" She searched herself, trying to define everything boiling inside of her. "I'm…angry."

He nodded but didn't interrupt.

"I'm angry at my mother for failing her daughters. I'm angry at myself for not seeing that I was making things worse with my sister." Now that she had started, that anger burned in her chest, making itself bigger. "I'm angry at Nora."

She bit back the rest because it didn't seem right to be angry with someone she had harmed. But Ripley wouldn't let her pull that punch. "Go on." he said evenly.

"I-I'm angry at Nora for running away from safety like a petulant child. How could she bolt from security? She had choices, I worked hard so she would have choices! I didn't want her to end up with no choices like…like me."

Her eyes stung, but she blinked away the tears that threatened. Now that the anger was flowing, she realized there had been a dam of it, pressure increasing for years.

"I hate that I'm helpless." She got up now and paced the room, back and forth, hands shaking at her sides. "I have built my entire life around not being helpless. Oh, it all makes me so angry! I want to…I want to…"

"Hit something," Ripley filled in softly.

Jane stopped pacing and stared at him. While she was a raging tempest, he was calm. There was no judgment in his suggestion, but there was a great deal of understanding. Of course there would be. He'd come from a background so similar to her own. He understood what it was like to grasp for even a whisper of control in a swirling sea of chaos.

"Yes," she admitted.

He pushed to his feet and began to unbutton his jacket. "Well, *that* I can help with."

~

What terrified Ripley about Jane's current state was that she didn't argue with him. She didn't question. After he'd suggested he could help her hit something, she had quietly done everything he'd asked. He was so accustomed to her taking a more active role in anything she did. He was so used to her asking questions.

To see her almost meek…no, that wasn't the right word for it. Desperate was more like it. She was so desperate to make this situation change that she would do anything he asked.

And he feared he couldn't save her. In the end, he might be just as helpless as she claimed to be.

He shook off those thoughts and focused instead on what they were about to do. He had stripped to only his trousers. She had removed her dress and slippers. Was it distracting to look at her in her short chemise, her pink stockings tied with velvet ribbon against her pale thighs?

Certainly. Was he going to do anything about it? Absolutely not. She needed a different kind of outlet at present.

"Normally I'd spend a little time explaining the basics of fighting," he said. "But you spent so much time at the club in Esme's corner that I think that might be sporting with your intelligence. So perhaps it would be better for you to show me what you recall."

She immediately shifted into a fighter's stance, her right leg slightly back, her hands fisted and up to block her face. He smiled.

"I'm impressed," he said. "Not that I ever doubted you. May I do a few adjustments?"

She arched a brow. "Just twenty-four hours ago, you had your tongue inside of me and now you're asking permission to touch my hands?"

He stepped up closer and looked down at her as he covered her fist with his palm and lifted it slightly. "I'm not the kind of man who takes without asking. Ever."

She'd been teasing him with her question, he knew, but now she stared up at him, her blue eyes softer. "Yes, that is very true. You are…remarkable Ripley. Cam."

He shivered at that little shift to the name that was only hers to whisper. She could have asked him for anything and he would have moved the world to give it to her. Perhaps he still would, before this was all finished. Whatever pain would follow when she pushed him away would be worth the little piece of heaven he was sharing with her now.

"You can't distract me with compliments," he said with a smile.

"I think I could," she teased back. "I think I could find ten different ways to distract you."

He shook his head. She was playing and he liked it. But he also saw it for what it was. He'd gotten too close, he'd seen her painful emotions too clearly. She wanted to build a wall. But he wouldn't let her.

Using all the control he had developed over years in the ring, he stepped back, put himself into a defensive position and raised his hands, palms flat, so she'd have something to hit.

"Tell me again what you're angry about," he said. "One punch for everything you say."

For a moment she seemed uncertain, but then she whispered, "I'm angry about my sister."

She threw a punch, weak but fully centered on his palm. He nodded. "Why?"

"Miss Knightly should have taken better care of her." She punched again, this time harder. "And Nora shouldn't have run." She punched again. "I hate that I'm afraid for her. I hate that I can't help her." She punched, this time a right left combination.

He nodded. "Very nice. Seems you learned a little from cornering."

"I did," she said. "I thought I might need it in the game."

"Go on," he encouraged. "What else?"

She swung again, her voice getting a little louder. "My mother," she said. "Her lies."

The punch was much harder now. It actually stung his palm. "Keep going."

"Losing Esme." She punched. "I miss her. I hate that I can't just be happy for her. I hate that she doesn't miss me."

Ripley frowned. He knew that wasn't true. Esme always talked about Jane when he saw her. But he understood Jane's feelings about being left behind. This wasn't about questioning or denying her those raw emotions. It was about allowing her to get them out so they wouldn't fester and infect.

"I hate the shop." She swung and it was wilder, as was her voice. "I hate it. It's boring and I don't belong there."

His brow wrinkled. He'd suspected as much the times he had come to see her there. Esme and Delacourt had meant well by offering Jane the chance at a different life, but Jane was only stifled by the repetitive monotony of such a place. She was a wildflower, but she'd been pushed into a hothouse.

"What else? Don't stop," he encouraged.

"I'm angry at myself." It was the hardest hit yet. "I'm ungrateful. I'm a bad sister. I'm an unappreciative friend. I'm a whore and everyone who sees me recognizes it, which is why I'll never succeed at the shop." Every cruel, untrue sentence was punctuated by a harder hit.

"More."

"I'm angry at you."

They both froze. Her eyes were wide, sparkling with unshed

tears. His heart was pounding and his throat felt thick. "Punch," he said. "Do it."

She swung, but this time it was weak when it struck his palm. Her breath was short and harsh.

"Why me?" he asked, keeping his tone gentle, not putting his own reaction into the question that meant everything in the world to him.

"Because…" Her hands dropped and her voice caught. "Because I can't. I-I *can't*, Ripley. And being near you makes me wish I was someone else."

He shut his eyes. He wanted to tell her everything in his heart in that moment. He wanted to tell her that he would never love the someone else she wanted to be as much as he loved her. That he would burn the world down for her smile, that he would bleed to save her from everyone who hurt her, even herself.

He wanted to throw himself on the fire of her and let himself burn. But this moment was about her feelings, not his. So he didn't do any of that. Instead he stepped closer, took the hands she'd dropped and lifted them up. He kissed each one gently.

"Jane Kendall, I'm glad you're you. Now, is there anything else you need to rage at?"

She laughed, but there was no pleasure to it. "I could rage at the world, but…not tonight. Doing that helped, just saying it helped."

"Sometimes you need to relieve some of the pressure." He motioned to the bed. "Are you ready?"

"After everything you could still…still want me?"

He started. "Of course I want you, Jane. There's nothing that could ever make me stop wanting you. But that wasn't what I had in mind. You're exhausted. And I think rest might be best for you. Especially since we'll ride hard to London tomorrow and go straight to Esme and Delacourt to see what they can tell us about this Hugo person."

She nodded and he could see the exhaustion line her face. She'd been trying to hide it from him. Old habit, he supposed, but God, how he wished she didn't feel she had to mask her true self even for a moment.

"Will you…will you stay with me?" she asked. "If you don't want to, I understand."

He caught her by the waist and drew her to him. She was soft in his arms, her bare skin warm against his. He held her close and reveled in the feel of her. "All I want in the world is to stay with you, Jane. Tonight. Tomorrow. Until you tire of me."

She buried her head against his chest with a shaky sigh and didn't resist when he moved her to the bed. She got into place and watched him as he blew out candles around the room. When he joined her, she tucked herself against him. He held her close, smoothing her hair until she drifted off to sleep.

And in the dark, in the quiet, he wondered if he would be able to truly help her once they reached London. And how long it would be before she tried to push him away because he'd seen too much of her soul.

CHAPTER 14

By the time they reached London the next evening, Jane had already built her walls back up. Oh, they sat close in the carriage. She spoke to him just as she always had. But Ripley was no fool. He had seen too much, she'd said too much. Now she would try to protect them both by inserting as much distance as she possibly could.

"When we stopped just outside the city, I asked the driver to take us straight to Esme and Delacourt's," he said.

She started, as if she'd forgotten he was in the carriage while she stared outside the window, her hands clutched together in her lap. Now she looked at him, her cheeks pinkening.

"Yes, thank you. The sooner we speak to them, the sooner we can find my sister."

She said the words with determination, but he knew her too well not to see the truth of her. Her little tells were subtle, she presented herself as steel to the world around her, but he saw the flickers of pain in her, of embarrassment and shame.

For the moment, he said nothing about it. Let her find the support she needed in her friends and it would calm her. And if she needed more? Well, he was here to provide it.

The carriage glided onto the drive at Delacourt's city estate. Jane took a deep breath and then exited the carriage with the assistance of one of the footmen who came rushing from the house. Ripley frowned. She'd been allowing him to help her for days and days, but even with this she separated herself a fraction.

Still, she did wait for him and took his arm, her fingers tightening around his bicep with a grip that spoke of her tension. Delacourt's butler welcomed them at the door.

"Ah, Miss Kendall," he said, all true friendliness. "We haven't seen you in a while, welcome."

"Thank you, Bentley," she said, her voice wavering slightly. "And you recall Mr. Ripley, I think."

"I do, indeed. The earls and countesses are gathered in the blue parlor. Please follow me and I'll announce you."

Her lips parted and she looked up at Ripley as they did as Bentley had asked. "They're not alone," she said softly.

He covered her hand with his. "Neither are you."

She came to a stop in the middle of the hallway and stared up at him. "Ripley," she murmured.

"My lords and ladies," Bentley called out at the door just a few feet in front of where they'd come to their sudden stop. "Miss Kendall and Mr. Ripley."

Ripley heard the happy murmur of voices within and guided Jane forward. They entered the room and he saw that, indeed, Esme and Delacourt weren't alone. The earl's sister, the Countess of Ramsbury, and her husband were also in attendance. And, as always, neither of them looked anything but pleased to see Jane.

Jane released his arm and stepped forward. "I-I'm sorry. I didn't know you'd be hosting company. We should have sent word."

Esme was already rushing forward and she wrapped her arms around Jane for a hard hug. "Gracious, don't get formal on me now! You know you're always welcome here, dearest." She glanced toward Ripley. "*Campbell.*"

He smiled despite the worry he felt for Jane. Esme had always cheekily called him Campbell as often as she did Ripley. Probably because it had always shocked those around him.

"Es," he said, and then turned toward the earls and Lady Ramsbury. "My lords. Lady Ramsbury."

He was greeted in a friendly enough way even though he noted that Delacourt stared from Jane to him and back again. Ripley liked Delacourt. He was sharp and direct, and he protected Esme with his whole heart. The same way Ripley wished to do with Jane.

Because that's what love was.

"You're pale," Esme said, pushing a lock of hair from Jane's forehead. "What is it?"

Jane glanced over her shoulder at Ripley and then at the rest of the room. "I-I need a moment with you. May we speak privately?"

"Of course." Esme wrapped an arm around her and tucked Jane into her side. Ripley could see Jane sag a little against her and he was glad she had support with Esme as much as with him. She needed all she could get. "We'll be back."

The two women left the room and Ripley let his breath out at last. Delacourt looked troubled as he watched the open door where they'd left. "Is Jane well?"

"No," Ripley said softly because now that he didn't have to put all his strength into her, he felt the full weight of his fears and heartbreak on her behalf.

Everyone in the room stared at him. And he knew in that moment that all his love for Jane was on his face. He couldn't hide it. He feared he'd never be able to hide it again.

Ramsbury squeezed his wife's hand and moved to pour Ripley a drink while Delacourt came to stand by him. The earl met his eyes, held there and there was only kindness and understanding within that focused expression. "Well, we will do anything we can to help her."

Ripley was glad he didn't ask for details. The ones about Jane's sister weren't his to share and his own feelings were too painful to name. He nodded. "Yes. Anything."

Because he would do anything for her. Even break his own heart.

~

Esme and Jane sat in front of the fire in Esme's massive library. Her friend hadn't stopped holding both her hands the entire time Jane had been confessing everything that had happened in the past few weeks. When she was finished, when she finally drew a shaky breath, Esme squeezed those hands gently.

"Oh, Jane. Why didn't you come to me at the beginning of all this?"

"And drag you back into the turmoil of my life? Of what and who I am?" Jane sighed.

"There is no dragging—"

"You got out, Esme," Jane interrupted. "You've made yourself the life you always belonged in, the life you deserve more than anyone in the world. I can't haul you back into the mud with me. I dragged poor Ripley into this and ruined him already."

"You haven't ruined Ripley."

Jane shut her eyes. "I've hauled him all over the countryside, exposed him to all my problems."

She could *feel* Esme's stare burning through her closed lids. "He's in love with you, Jane."

Jane flinched. There it was, said out loud, harder to shove aside than when the knowledge of it was just a refrain in her head every time he looked at her.

"I know," she whispered. "I know he is."

"When you love someone, their mud is your mud. And it's worth getting down in it, worth fighting to come out of it together. I'd rather be covered in mud next to Finn than clean without him."

Jane stared at her friend. Esme had fled the life of a lady, run from a dangerous fiend who threatened her. She'd fit herself into Jane's world, but in truth she'd never really belonged there. When

Delacourt appeared, it had been evident that she would be loved. And Jane knew from personal experience that no one loved as fiercely and loyally as Esme did in return.

"But I'm not you," she said. "I can't offer him anything of value."

"Except your beautiful, strong, loving heart." Esme cupped her cheeks. "Which is worth all the rubies and diamonds and pearls in this silly kingdom."

"Well, now you're just being ridiculous," Jane said, and smiled despite herself. "Ripley is a situation I cannot even think about right now. Not until I find Nora. Will you help me?"

Esme nodded. "Of course. Though I do wonder why you also kept your sister a secret from me all the years we lived together."

Jane shrugged. "Talking about her hurt. All of it hurts."

"Oh, Jane," Esme whispered, and wrapped and arm around her. She hugged her gently. "Why don't we go back to the others? It's more likely that Finn, Sebastian and Marianne would recognize who this Hugo person might be than me. I lost track of all those fops when I left this life and I can hardly be bothered to figure them all out now. Poor Bentley has to give me a cheat sheet every time we can manage to get a few of them to lower themselves to come to our home."

Jane's cheeks burned at the idea, but she nodded as Esme got up and Jane followed her back down the hallway to the parlor. She'd long ago given up on the idea of humiliation and yet that was what burned in her chest as they returned to the others.

Ripley immediately made his way back to her and the relief she felt when he did was too powerful. She focused on him while Esme very kindly took the others aside and briefly explained what was going on so that Jane wouldn't have to repeat the awful story all over again.

"They'll think me a fool," Jane said as she stared into his eyes and allowed their depths to calm her.

Ripley shrugged. "Then they can all go to hell."

She smiled at his instant dismissal of people who mattered in the world and in his business. Because she needed to feel him, she took his hand, memorized the rough slide of his palm against hers. He squeezed gently and she drew a ragged breath.

"I'm so sorry, Jane," Delacourt said as the others faced them at last. She searched his face for annoyance that she'd brought this mess to his house, but saw none. In fact, he crossed to her and touched her shoulder briefly. There was nothing but kindness in him as he said, "Please know that we'll do all in our power to find your sister."

"Thank you."

"Esme told us about this man who was involved," Ramsbury said, and he, too, looked nothing but supportive when he spoke to her. "But I'd like to hear all the details you have directly from you and Ripley."

Jane drew a ragged breath and tried to organize the snippets of information that banged around in her head constantly. "The girl at my sister's school said they were going to elope. And my mother's letter to Nora called him Hugo and said his grandfather is titled. That's all the information I have."

She glanced at Ripley, and like he had read her mind, he withdrew it from the inside pocket of his jacket, smoothed it and handed it over.

Delacourt glanced at it, then surprised Jane by giving it to Marianne rather than Sebastian. Esme joined her sister-in-law and together the two women read over it, heads close together.

"So the grandson of a titled gentleman," Marianne said, her gaze never leaving the letter, like she was trying to decipher some code it held.

"Yes," Jane said. Her humiliation was fading at the kindness of those in the room. "Obviously he might have been lying to my sister about that fact. We've no idea."

"It's possible," Esme said with a quick glance up at her. "But I think we start from the idea that every fact we have is true. We can adjust that belief if we find evidence to the contrary. Did the girl actually call him young?"

Jane nodded. "Yes. She said young man."

"Then he's probably around her age, or not much older," Delacourt mused. "Because when you're seventeen or eighteen, anyone at the top end of their twenties looks old and over thirty is ancient."

"I resent that," Ramsbury muttered, and the others chuckled. He glanced at Jane with a smile. "I just celebrated my thirtieth birthday."

She smiled along with them, her tangled emotions soothed by their easiness. Jane had only known them all in passing, had never thought she'd bring something so emotional to the doorstep of an earl and his very important family. And yet she felt no judgment. No cruelty. No wonder Esme loved them all so fiercely.

"And his name is Hugo," Marianne said, tapping a finger to her lip. "A somewhat uncommon name."

"Hugo, Hugo," Delacourt repeated, and looked at Ramsbury. "There's Stopford."

"Yes, but he's a viscount," Ramsbury said.

"And the grandson of a duke."

"I don't know." Ramsbury shook his head. "If the young man, himself, was titled, why would Jane's mother reference the grandfather and not the son, himself?"

"I think Ramsbury is correct," Esme said. "There's a specificity to the language."

Jane nodded. "In my world, a viscount would be a fine catch all on his own. My mother would crow about a viscount, and if he would one day inherit a dukedom? She would have been telling my sister to land him at all costs."

"So an *untitled* grandson," Delacourt said. "Probably. With the first name of Hugo."

"Hugo Fielding?" Ramsbury suggested.

"He's hardly young," Delacourt said. "He's pushing fifty. Oh, what about Bernard Horne's grandson? Isn't he a Hugo?"

"But Horne isn't titled," Ramsbury said. "He acts like an entitled prick, but that's just his nature. No title."

"Damn." Delacourt sighed. "We must have a copy of Debrett's around here somewhere. Or we can get one. I'm sure we'll figure it out."

"What about Eldon Granger?" Marianne said, and glanced at the two men.

"Oh, yes!" Esme said. "I recall him. His middle name was Hugo and he went by that."

"He was always coming around Claudia and me against the wall," Marianne said. "That's why I thought of him. And his grandfather is the Duke of Hightower. He's the youngest son of…oh, what was his name. I'll think of it." She pondered for a moment and then her face lit up. "Pottinger!"

Jane jerked her face toward Ripley as she realized why that name was instantly familiar. She clung tighter to his hand even as all the color left his face and he staggered back a step.

"Pottinger," he gasped. "The Earl of Pottinger?"

"Ripley," Jane whispered, and smoothed her fingers over the top of his hand. "Breathe…please breathe."

"Yes, that's right," Delacourt said. All of them were staring at Ripley now, his strong reaction too much to ignore. "What does that name mean to you?"

"He…" Ripley trailed off and swallowed a few times before he said, "The Earl of Pottinger is my father."

CHAPTER 15

Ripley's mind was spinning, or was the room spinning? He was too flummoxed to tell the difference in that moment. All he knew was that everyone was staring at him, worried, wondering…

And then there was Jane, her hand still in his, her soft voice encouraging with words he couldn't quite grasp as his father's name echoed in his mind over and over.

He realized she had guided him to the settee and she tugged him down and lifted her hands to his cheeks. They were cool on his heated skin, her gaze firm on his. Everything calmed with her at the center.

"I'm sorry," he gasped out. "I wasn't expecting that."

"Of course you weren't," Jane said.

Delacourt stepped closer. "Pottinger is your father?" he asked gently.

Ripley looked up at him. Both this man and Ramsbury held the same rank in Society as his father. What would they think of him now? But did it matter? Jane needed him to push past the negative feelings that boiled inside of him and focus. So for her, he did.

"Yes. I'm his illegitimate son." He arched a brow, ready to face some kind of interrogation or cruelty.

It was Ramsbury who replied first. "I see."

It was said so softly, so lightly. It almost felt like pity. He cleared his throat and withdrew his hands from Jane's. "So this Eldon person. My half-brother. He seems to match all the items we know about whoever was involved with Nora."

"What kind of—" Jane began, and then cut herself off. She glanced at Ripley and he realized she was trying to protect him. Thinking of him rather than her sister.

"Ask whatever you wish to ask," he said. "We need to know."

She shook her head. "This is too much, though. I can see it."

"It's not," he said. Lied because it was. But he loved her enough to endure it.

She faced the others. "What sort of man is he, then? Marianne, you said you knew him."

"He was always very quiet, almost a wallflower in his own right. I didn't think much of him one way or another, but he never seemed cruel or calculating."

Marianne glanced at Ripley as she spoke, but he could tell she answered the question honestly. He doubted the kind countess could be anything *but* honest.

There was a fraction of relief on Jane's face. "That's something then." She looked at the two earls. "Do either of you know him well enough to reach out? Or...or to his father or grandfather?"

Ramsbury and Delacourt exchanged a look. "They're both so much older," Delacourt said. "I think that set found the two of us rather foolish."

"And with reason," Ramsbury said with a faint smile. "But I suppose I could make some inquiries and make a meeting—"

Ripley rose to his feet. "No. I'll do it. I'll reach out to my father, myself."

Jane followed him up. "No! Cam, no, you've done enough."

She had used his first name and it fit. This was, after all, the most intimate of moments when he was stripped down to the heart of who he was. The heart of his pain and his past and his loss. He could see the use of that name wasn't lost on the others, either.

"We'll leave you a moment," Delacourt said, and the couples stepped from the room. Marianne closed the door behind them.

Now that they were alone, Ripley stared down into those beautiful dark blue eyes, rimmed with unshed tears and regrets. "She's your sister," he said softly.

"You can't." She shook her head. "You can't. I know you don't want to see him—speak to him—after all he did to you and to your mother."

She wasn't wrong and he wouldn't lie or deny it. That would be sporting with her intelligence. "For you?" he said instead. "For you I'd do anything, Jane. You know that."

Her expression twisted before she bent her head. She rested her forehead against his chest with a shuddering sigh. "Even if it destroys you."

"Yes," he said. They stood that way, quiet for a long moment. Then he drew a shuddering sigh. "Let me send a message to him and see if he'll even receive me. He's been fairly quiet since the last time he sent me a message and I wrote *Fuck Off Tosser* on it and sent it back." He shook his head at how wide her eyes went. "But we'll see."

She nodded. "Thank you and…and I'm sorry."

He cupped her face, loving the slide of her soft skin through his rougher hands. Loving how she tilted her face toward his without hesitation. Like she was his. Like he was hers. He bent his head and touched his lips to hers.

She wrapped her arms around his neck without hesitation and opened to him. He didn't take. Oh, he felt passion rise in him, of course. Just being near her did that and would do that until the moment he took his last breath. But this was about comfort. His to her, but also hers to him. He took her in, reveling in her warmth and her presence and everything that gave him the peace he'd been looking for his whole violent life.

They parted at last and he withdrew from her arms with difficulty. He smiled at her, hoping it would give her comfort, that he could somehow show her he was fine with all this. Of course he wasn't. And yet he would still do it and accept whatever consequences would come.

~

When Jane called for the others to return to the room a few moments later, all she saw was their kindness. Their support. It was odd that it was harder to see that for herself, but she was grateful Ripley had found it. He knew these men, after all. Depended on their patronage. It seemed he wouldn't lose it. Perhaps he would even gain a deeper friendship by the time it was all over.

Ripley cleared his throat. "I appreciate your kindness," he said to the group at large. "I wonder if I might ask for a bit more of it. Delacourt, may I send a message from here?"

Her lips parted. "You're sending the message to the earl now?"

"The duty won't get any easier the longer I wait. And we'll be more likely to have a response the sooner I do." His voice was rough as he spoke. Pained.

Delacourt nodded. "Of course. I'll take you to my study and give you materials and some privacy."

Marianne approached Ramsbury and touched his arm. Their eyes met, silent communication flowing between them. Jane flinched. She recognized that she had the same with Ripley. That was love, wasn't it? Just knowing another person without having to say a word.

"I think we'll leave you," Ramsbury said. "But Ripley, if you need anything at all, please don't hesitate."

Ripley looked at him with gratitude plain on his face before he shook the earl's hand. Delacourt did the same, then kissed his sister's cheek before he motioned for Ripley to follow him.

Esme squeezed Jane's hand before she led Marianne and Ramsbury away for their own farewells. Jane drew a shaky breath when she was left alone. This felt like a storm she couldn't hold back now. Everything would crash down soon, for better or for worse.

Esme returned to the room and wrapped an arm around her. Together they walked to the window and watched the Ramsbury carriage make its way from the drive and into the busy street. "Why don't you two stay for supper after the message is sent?"

Jane glanced at her and the words bubbled up with her hardly knowing she was about to speak them. "I hate the shop."

Esme blinked. "That's an unexpected response to an invitation."

"I'm sorry." Jane shook her head. "I know I'm horribly ungrateful, but I watched Ripley be so brave in confessing his truth, I knew I had to share my own."

Esme nodded slowly. "I'm glad you did. I know it's very different from anything you ever knew."

"It's *tedious*," Jane admitted. "And I live in terror that someone who knew me before will come in. It happened already. Elizabeth Bowerton."

Her friend pulled a look. "Oh, I remember her. Nasty thing."

"She wasn't always, sometimes she was more when we were together. But she was dreadful when she realized it was me behind that counter." Jane sighed. "I wasted your charity, I fear. But I hope you can ultimately sell the place. Make some of it back."

"If you don't wish to continue there, then I'd never force you," Esme said. "But what will you do instead to support yourself? Perhaps support your sister when you find her?"

Now the truth would have to be shared. The pain begun. "I think I'll…leave London," Jane said softly. "Get a small place with the little I have left. I could do some kind of servant's work. Fake the references and I'm sure I could find that."

"You think that would be less boring?" Esme asked gently.

Jane looked toward the door. "Probably not. But it would be less dangerous."

"I don't think you're talking about former lovers now. Or standing at a counter waiting for customers."

"No."

Esme said nothing in response to that, just let Jane ponder the statement.

At last Jane sighed. "I *adore* you. I adore him. But I can only hurt you by staying. I already have. It's what I do." She held up a hand when Esme took a big breath to retort. "Please don't argue. I'm so tired of arguing. Just let me go if that's what I decide to do."

Esme's eyes were filled with rare tears as she gripped Jane's hand. "You saved my life more than once. So did he. I want you both to be happy and I believe with all my heart that you could be together. But I also know that you've spent a great deal of time having to do what others wanted. I would never stop you from following the path you thought was right. But I will love you like the sister you are to me whether you hide from me or not. And I won't be the only one."

Jane shivered. The fact of that felt so raw, but she was saved from having to respond when Ripley returned to the parlor, Delacourt at his heels. Jane forced some brightness to her face.

"You were quick."

He shrugged and she hated how all the color was gone from his cheeks. "I didn't have much to say. Just a simple…well, perhaps not-so-simple, request."

"I've invited you and Jane to supper," Esme said without releasing Jane's hand, even though she held it far more gently. "And she has refused to answer."

Ripley looked at her and then he shook his head slightly. "I appreciate the kindness, Es. I do. But I wouldn't be good company right now."

Esme released Jane and moved to Delacourt. He put an arm around her, his faced lined with concern for his wife. For Jane and for Ripley, too. But Esme's voice was steady as she said, "I understand. Please tell us if you need anything."

Ripley nodded absently and motioned for the door. The carriage he had let remained a little ways back on the drive. It rolled forward as they made their way out the door and Ripley said something to the driver as Jane hugged Esme. She felt the tremble in her friend.

"Please don't do anything rash, love," Esme whispered. "And never run away without telling me."

"I never would," Jane promised. She squeezed Delacourt's hand with true gratitude for all he'd done and continued to do. When she turned, she let the Delacourt footman help her into the rig. She watched as Delacourt shook Ripley's hand and then Esme lifted up to kiss his cheek. She said something to him, too soft for Jane to hear. His expression softened a fraction.

"Thank you, Es," he said, and then he followed Jane into the carriage. Soon they rolled through the busy London streets together. She didn't ask where he was taking her, but it didn't matter. All she could think about was her sister, all she could think about was how Ripley would cut himself open for her. Her two failures, pressed tightly together now, showing her that she could only cause pain to those she loved.

Eventually they pulled up to the club and he helped her down. He spoke to the driver as she stood before the big, double doors leading into the fine life he had created. At last the man drove away, taking the rig Ripley had probably spent far too much letting for her. All for her. All this loss for her.

She followed him into the club. It was empty save for Brentwood, who was tidying up for the end of the day. When they stepped in, he stopped and looked from Ripley to her and back again.

"Good to have you back," he said, and then nodded to Jane. "Miss Kendall."

"Mr. Brentwood," she said, hating that heat filled her cheeks. Did she actually care what this man thought of her? Of course she did. He was important to Ripley.

"Any trouble?" Ripley asked, his voice rough even as he crossed to shake Brentwood's hand.

"None," Brentwood said. "One or two groused you weren't here this week, but I matched them with the best at sparring and they started focusing on not getting their heads knocked off instead."

Ripley flashed a grin she realized she hadn't seen in at least a day. That carefree, wicked expression she had always been drawn to. Her heart thudded at its return, and it broke with the realization that all her drama had been the reason for its absence.

"Good. Then they'll be very pleased to have me back once I'm finished with my current issues." He glanced at Jane and she ducked her head.

"Well, I'm available to run them ragged as long as you need. Are you out again?" Brentwood asked.

"It depends. I'm waiting on a missive."

"Speaking of which…" Brentwood stepped off and returned with a small stack of letters and cards. He handed them over. "I think you might have a new member coming, judging from that one on top: Pottinger. He seems a bit old to take up fisticuffs, but he has two sons, I think. Both of an age to—"

He stopped as Ripley dropped the rest of the post and tore open the seal on the folded sheets from his father. Jane rushed to him, grasping his arm as he opened the papers with shaking hands.

Brentwood stared at them, then inclined his head. "I'll be here tomorrow, Ripley. I'll take care of everything until you're back. Good evening, Miss Kendall."

He left then, though neither of them acknowledged it.

"How could he reply so swiftly?" she gasped.

Ripley shrugged. "He doesn't live far from Delacourt. If he responded immediately, sent his fastest runners—" He stopped and drew a shaky breath.

She smoothed her palm over his arm. "What does he say?"

Ripley's face was pale as he handed over the letter. "He wants to see me first thing in the morning."

She read the few lines.

Mr. Ripley,

I very much look forward to seeing you tomorrow at nine a.m. We have a great deal to discuss.

Pottinger

She found her heart sinking at the cool tone of the note. "He isn't exactly warm, is he?"

Ripley shrugged. "My mother used to speak of him as loving when they first started together. Kind. But the kind of man who could abandon the mother of his child completely, let her scrap and die the way she did…"

She caught his hand in hers. "I'm sorry."

He shook his head. "You keep saying that as if you created this monster."

"I did," she insisted. "You never would have had to see or speak to this man again if it weren't for me and my wayward sister I couldn't even keep track of. So *yes*, I take responsibility for that, Ripley."

He traced her cheek with a fingertip. "Will you come up with me? Come to my home and my kitchen and my bed?"

She shut her eyes briefly. It was so easy to picture being in all those places forever. She nodded. "Yes. And I'm also coming with you tomorrow."

His eyes widened. "Jane, you don't have to do that. I don't know how pleasant this is going to be or how he'll even receive you."

"I unleashed this wave of catastrophe, Ripley. If you don't think I'll stand by your side to keep you from drowning, you're a fool."

The corner of his lip twitched. "You wouldn't be the first one to call me a fool. And yes, it would be easier to have you there. I suppose it would be easier for you, too, since you wouldn't have to wait and wonder what was happening."

He offered his arm and she took it. Together they went upstairs. The first time she'd come into his home above the club, she had been hysterical, terrified. She hadn't really looked at where this man made his home. She smiled as he shed his jacket and rolled up his sleeves.

"You're cooking again?"

"I'm out of fire and brimstone," he teased, reminding her of what she'd said to him that first night she'd come to him with her terror over her sister.

"May I look around your rooms while you do? I want to see the lair of the great Campbell Ripley. See where the Dragon keeps his horde."

He nodded. "Look away. I've no secrets from you."

He kissed her temple and then left her for the kitchen. She watched him go, watched the sleek movements of that wonderful body. How could a man be such a hulk of muscle and flesh and yet be so graceful, she would never know.

But she'd been given carte blanche to explore and so she did. She stepped into the parlor first. It was a small room but cozy, despite the chill from no fires being lit for a few days. She lit a lamp to carry with her and examined the room. The furniture there was mismatched but appeared comfortable.

There were two chairs before the fire and she could picture sitting in them at night. He would read to her. Perhaps she'd become brave enough to read out to him. He'd never tease her about her mistakes or mispronunciations. Maybe one day she'd even get bold enough to admit she'd learned to read because she'd wanted to keep his little notes and letters to her private. Just hers. A tiny piece of him that no one else could take.

She blinked. What was she thinking? The future wasn't in this room. And yet she didn't stop her tour. She found a study next. The desk was big, piled with papers and letters and accounts. This was clearly where he managed the business of the club at night. She moved around, looking at his even handwriting, recalling every time he'd written her name over the years.

Jane. My Janie.

She also noted a portrait above the fire on the desk. She moved to it and lifted her lantern to see it better. It was a woman and judging from the dark eyes that she knew so well, she thought it was Ripley's mother. One of the paintings by her former protector, it seemed, and a beautiful one. Jane smiled. Regina Ripley had been so very pretty and she had a kind expression. Sad, perhaps, but very kind. Sometimes she saw that same look on her son's face. The same little wrinkle to his forehead.

Once again, it was too easy to think about being comfortable here. Perhaps she would help him organize his paperwork better. She'd sit at the window while he worked, talking to him about his day. He'd pour her tea...or whisky. Or both. She smiled at the thought before she once again shoved it away. This look into his life was too dangerous, it seemed.

She stepped from that room and went to the end of the hallway. There was a short staircase there and it led up to a third floor that had two doors. She opened the first, a small bedchamber, though the furniture was all covered with sheets.

The last door she hesitated at. This was his bedroom. She knew it, and though she had made full use of her freedom to explore, going into this chamber felt different. Her hand shook as she turned the knob and stepped inside.

It was a big chamber, though simply appointed. A door to one side likely led to his dressing room. Beside it was a small table adorned with some writing implements. There were two chairs before the fire with another table between them where a few books were stacked.

And then there was the bed. Their encounters before this had been in smaller beds in inns. But this bed was different, bigger, laid with a soft coverlet that she traced her fingers along until she reached the pillow where the man she loved placed his head each night.

"Fuck," she muttered under her breath, and then turned to the cold fireplace. She set her lamp aside and set a fire, tending it until it came to life to warm the room for him later. That was the least she could do after everything he'd done for her in these last weeks.

She was just finishing up when she heard Ripley clear his throat from the door behind her. She faced him and found him staring at her and then at the flames.

"You set a fire?"

She nodded, even though her cheeks burned. To do that was a simple act, but one of love. Now it felt like she was under scrutiny.

He stared for a second more and then shook his head. "Supper is ready, though it isn't much."

"I'm sure it will be perfect," she assured him.

Together they returned to the kitchen and the simple table there that he'd set for them. He'd roasted some vegetables that smelled like heaven and there was bread and cheese.

"As I said, not much since I haven't been home," he said as he pulled back her chair and helped her in.

"I cannot wait," she assured him, and smiled up at him as he filled her plate.

He sat across from her and did the same for himself. But when she started eating, he didn't. He moved his food around, but he was quiet and hardly raised the fork to his lips.

After a few moments like that, she covered his hand and squeezed gently. "You must be worried about meeting with your father tomorrow."

He lifted his gaze to her. "That wasn't what I was thinking about." His voice was rough, low.

She wrinkled her brow. "No?"

"Jane...Jane, I love you."

CHAPTER 16

Ripley understood something about the idea of pressure. He'd faced a great deal of it in his life. He knew that if it got too high, whatever it surged against would burst. And that was what had just happened as he sat at his table across from Jane. The words he'd kept silent in his heart for years had finally pressed too hard. Burned too bright. He'd had to say them, there was no escaping it.

And now she stared at him, her eyes bright with a joy that was unmistakable. A joy that faded even as she drew her hand away from his.

"Please don't say that," she whispered.

He shook his head. He'd never thought she'd accept that. At least not immediately. Her difficult life gave her too many reasons to fear it. And yet he had no energy to deny the truth anymore, not to protect himself from rejection. Not to protect her from whatever terror those words inspired.

"But I must," he said. "All I want is you. All I dream of is you. I know that frightens you. Hell, it scares me, too. But there it is."

She bent her head and he could see her struggle. The fight that was within her was as clear as any he had taken in a ring. Would he win? He hoped so. He hoped that she'd find the strength to tell him she loved him, too, even if she still believed that wasn't enough.

But she didn't. Her hands fell into her lap beneath the table and she didn't speak, just looked down at her half-full plate. It was disappointing. And yet he still understood it.

"Will you stay with me tonight?" he asked. "Just be with me."

Her gaze lifted and found his. Of course it would. Giving her body to him had become a way that was comfortable to her. She understood it, felt she could control it. And if that was the only way she would pour out whatever feelings she had for him, the only way she would accept the ones that burned in him for her...well, he'd take it.

"Yes," she whispered, and stood. She leaned across the table and cupped his cheek, her fingers so soft against the rough stubble there. She bent in and kissed him.

He couldn't hold back the groan that shuddered from his lips at that touch. How had he resisted it for so long? Now he craved this woman like he craved the food at that rough table. He wanted her like his lungs wanted air.

Even as he continued to kiss her, he stood, tugging her around the table, up against his chest. Her arms wound around him, she flattened her body to his and they stood there together for what felt like an eternity just kissing.

At last, though, she pulled away a fraction. She looked up into his face, almost in wonder, like she was seeing him for the first time. Her breath was shallow as she murmured, "Let's go to your room."

He nodded and clasped her hand, tangling his fingers in hers as he led her from the kitchen, back up the narrow staircase and into the room she had prepared for them. The fire she had laid had warmed it and he smiled as he tugged her into the chamber and shut the door.

She pressed her back to it and he caged her in with his hands on either side of her head. She lifted her chin, offering her mouth to him, but he didn't take it. He just looked at her, this slip of a woman who had tangled herself so fully in every part of him. His Janie.

"You are so beautiful," he said.

She opened her eyes and looked up at him. "So are you."

He laughed. "You keep saying that. I almost think you believe it."

"I do believe it," she said. "Because it's true. The most beautiful man I've ever known." She lifted her hands to his cravat and began to untie it.

He shuddered, both at the touch and also at the words. She might not say she loved him, but he knew she did. That didn't mean she would allow them to be together once this situation with her sister was resolved. But she loved him.

She unwound the cravat and tugged it away. She held it up, pulling it taut between her hands. He smiled as he thought of the night she'd bound his hands so he wouldn't be allowed to take over. When she tossed the scrap of fabric aside, it was an act of trust. To have earned that from a woman who was more likely to be suspicious was powerful.

"Will you take off the rest, please?" she asked.

"So polite," he chuckled, and pushed off the door to back up a step. He was quick as he removed his waistcoat, his shirt. He had expected her to undress, as well, but she remained pressed to the door, just watching him unwrap himself. So he slowed down, let her anticipate as he unfastened his trousers and slowly parted them.

She licked her lips and he was almost undone without even touching her.

"Fuck me, Jane," he grunted.

"That's the idea," she whispered back.

It was all playful and wicked, but when she finally stepped forward and extended a hand to touch his bare chest, dragging her fingers up, sliding them along his jawline and finally into his hair, she was gentle. She pulled him down to her, brushing her lips back and forth across his like it was the first time.

He whispered her name against her mouth and pushed his hands into the silky mass of her hair. She shivered and pressed her fingers into his back, nails lightly raking the skin and creating ricochets of sensation through every nerve ending in his body.

He wanted to say that he loved her again, but instead he moved his mouth to her throat. He traced the words there, showing her instead of telling her. Wanting her to feel it in the way they connected physically. Perhaps that was all she would accept for now. All she would understand.

And so they moved together, slower now, gentle. He found the buttons along the front of her gown and unfastened them without moving his lips from her throat. She whimpered her pleasure as he parted the dress and slid his fingers inside, along the lacy edge of her chemise.

"Please," she murmured against his mouth.

He lifted his gaze to hers, holding there as he peeled the dress away and left it in a pile at her feet. He did the same with her chemise and reveled in the fact that they were naked together. Every time it happened, it was like magic. Tonight he wanted to savor it and her. They'd both earned that after all the pain. And it would sustain him, and he hoped her, through whatever was to come.

"I don't want to hurry," he said. "I have all night for this, Jane. So you're not going to rush me."

A little light of defiance came into her eyes. "I could."

"You could," he agreed. "But I'm asking you not to."

Her lips parted and then she softened. "I won't."

Once again, that confession of love returned to his lips. Now that he'd said it, he wanted to keep saying it. As if she sensed that, she stepped closer. She lifted up on her tiptoes and kissed him, drowning out the words and the thoughts and leaving only her and the way her body felt when it brushed his.

That would be enough for the night. It had to be.

～

Jane was fighting a losing battle in Ripley's arms. In her life as a lightskirt, she'd always had tactics and techniques to keep herself from becoming too attached to any man. Ways to separate herself, never give everything. But with this man?

Well, she'd never been able to do it. From the first time they'd talked to the first time they'd made love she'd felt her defenses chipping away. And now they were almost gone entirely, finally stripped bare by his raw confession that he loved her.

She felt that love even now as he let his hands smooth over her with such gentle care. Such easy pleasure. He swept her up and she gasped with surprise, breaking their kiss. He carried her like a bridegroom might have over to his bed. She was put to mind of the night she'd come here to ask for help with Nora. He'd carried her to his rooms then, too, but for a far less pleasurable purpose. Though his care for her, his gentle protection when she couldn't bear her own weight, that had been just as impactful.

Tonight, though, he set her on his bed, dragging his fingers along the lines of her body as he released her. She opened her arms and legs to him, beckoning him to join her, but he didn't. For a moment he just stood over her, outlined in firelight, and looked at her.

"What are you doing?" she asked.

"Memorizing this moment. You spread out in my bed, like I've imagined so many times since that first moment I saw you."

She sat up a little on her elbows, arched her back a tiny bit. If there was one thing she knew, it was how to fulfill a man's fantasy. Doing it for this man was nothing but pleasure.

"Have you memorized it enough?" she asked. He nodded and she smiled as she reached for his hand, drew him down toward her. "Good, because I doubt the only thing you imagined was staring at me all night."

He covered her and they relaxed back together. His weight on her was heaven, pressing her into the soft coverlet, a reminder of all his strength, his power, his control.

It made those moments when she stole all that all the more meaningful.

Somehow she expected him to just take her. She was ready for him, after all. The moment he touched her, she was always ready, slick with wanting, trembling with need. But he didn't. He went back to kissing her, just as gently and thoroughly as he had in the kitchen. She tangled one hand into his thick hair and with the other she traced the muscles of his back as she allowed herself to sink into the pleasure of just kissing this man. She felt the hardness of his cock pressing heavy against her thigh, and yet there was still no rush to him.

Once again, she was reminded of both how different he was from any other man in her life, and also of how deeply and powerfully she loved him. That he loved her in return was both pleasure and pain.

"Don't think," he whispered against her lips.

She shivered at the idea that he could tell she was doing just that. That he knew her so well. She pulled back a little and smiled at him, wicked. But not because she wanted to use that wickedness as a wall, only because he inspired it.

"Then do all those things you do so well to make me stop thinking," she said softly.

He flashed a grin down at her, his chuckle racing up her spine and making her body grip like it was seeking his.

"With great pleasure," he murmured, kissed her once more and then guided his lips down her neck.

He sucked and nipped, taking his time, savoring her. She pushed away all her worries about him, about her sister, about the pain surely to come and separate them. She focused entirely on this moment, this man, this pleasure.

It was easy when he provided so much. He had learned her in the desperate, passionate time they had shared recently. He took that knowledge now and put it to good use. When he sucked one nipple, she arched beneath him with a little cry. He smiled against her, she felt the shift of his lips, and that made it even better. Her pleasure was his pleasure and that was the most erotic thing she'd ever felt.

So much so that she wished to share it.

She lifted beneath him, cupping his cheek, tilting his face away from her skin so that he looked at her. That moment nearly brought her to tears. The firelight hit him just so, outlining all the imperfections of his scar, the crookedness of his nose, all the things that made him so damned beautiful. She caught her breath and said, "I want to give you the same pleasure you give me."

He chuckled. "Can't give over control for even a moment, eh?"

"I've given you plenty of control for plenty of moments," she corrected. "Why don't we surrender control together?"

He arched that scarred brow. "What do you have in mind?"

"Come up here. Lie on the pillows." She scooted to the side and let him do just that. She rolled into him, kissing him, lazy at first and then with more purpose. She almost forgot what she wanted to do as she was swept away on the waves of him. But then she forced herself back to the moment. She pulled away and smiled at his grumpy frown before she began to inch down his body, just as he had with hers.

He watched her, hands pressed against his sides, like he was trying to keep himself from taking over. She smiled as she flicked her tongue over a nipple. He gasped in response, just as she always did when he did the same. But she didn't linger long. She slid farther down, tracing the muscles of his stomach, the ridge of his hip. And then she arrived at the very impressive cock. She caught him in hand and stroked once, twice.

His back bowed and he let out a great moan. The power of that was wickedly addictive and there was a moment when she wanted nothing more than to suck him dry and then crow in triumph that she could best a champion. But she didn't. She'd promised mutual surrender and she intended to have it.

Once she figured out how to best manage it, that was. He was so much taller than she was now that she was leaning over him, she realized what she had in mind would be difficult to align. Then the fix hit her.

"Will you slide up on the bed a little?"

His eyes widened. "Are you intending to…"

She nodded. "Oh yes. Most definitely."

He moved so fast that his cock bounced out of her hand. She laughed at his ardor and he smiled down at her in turn. It was such a remarkable thing that even in the midst of what was a fraught, emotional situation in every way, he could make things so…easy. The only person in her life to have ever done so.

She pivoted, settling herself onto his chest so that she faced his cock. He smoothed a hand over her bare arse before he grabbed her hips and maneuvered her.

"Oh, this is a fine view," he drawled. "You arse-up in my lap, that sweet little pussy just perfect for devouring."

"Then devour away, Cam," she murmured. "If you can maintain enough focus."

She lowered her mouth to him and swirled her tongue around his length. He swore loud and long, but then he wrapped an arm around her hips to hold her in place, spread her open with two fingers, and licked her in return.

She bucked back and he laughed. "Oh, we'll see who can focus."

They were silent after that, both giving everything they had to pleasing the other. As he nipped and licked and sucked her clitoris, she swirled her tongue around him, taking him as far as he would go into her throat. She was drunk on his taste, addled by the way he tensed beneath her. And addled in return by his expert mouth. He knew every route to her pleasure. They were well-traveled roads for him by now and he didn't neglect a one. Soon she was bucking back, sucking him with less finesse as the waves of pleasure increased and then overwhelmed.

She moaned around him and then let him fall from her lips. Pleasure bordered on pain as he tormented her, lapping her up like she was the finest wine, forcing her to give and give until she flopped down against his legs, still shaking from release.

She fought to catch her breath, to refocus on doing to him what he'd just done to her. But before she could, he caught her hips and flipped her over onto her back. He shifted over her, pushing his hips between her thighs.

"Oh, Cam, I wanted to—"

"I know," he interrupted. "But I need this. I need you."

There was something so real in that statement. So true. He *needed* her. And there was no way she could ever deny him. She didn't want to.

"Ready for me?" he whispered, always seeking consent no matter what she had already willingly, enthusiastically surrendered. Yet another thing to adore about him.

She pulled him in for a kiss, tasting her release on his tongue. "All my life," she murmured back.

His kiss deepened at that admission. They both knew what she meant, even if she couldn't say the words he wanted to hear. The words she knew would hurt him as much as they pleased him.

He shifted and the hard head of him nudged her. She lifted and he took her in one slick slide. He gathered her closer, clutching her like she was something precious he never wanted to lose. He delved deep into her still-quivering body, his hips rolling against hers, hitting her sensitive clitoris with each thrust. She met him, moaning his name over and over between kisses as the pleasure he had just given rose all over again. This time quicker and sharper thanks to her earlier release.

When she came, he pulled back, watching her as she writhed beneath him. There was no show this time, no playful teasing with her reactions as she'd done at the beginning of this night. No, there was no choice but to give everything to him then, all that she was, all that she had.

It was only when the waves shortened, when her breath slowed a fraction that he dropped his forehead to hers and thrust a little harder. This was for his pleasure now, finally after all he'd given. She gripped him with every thrust, trying to return what she'd received. She felt him balance on the edge and then he fell, gloriously, powerfully, with a roaring cry that seemed to shake the very room.

For a brief moment, she wished he would come inside of her. Fill her with himself, merge them entirely. But he didn't. He withdrew and spent between them. He collapsed over her, his breath shaky against her skin.

She held him close in the quiet dark, smoothing his flexing muscles, their panting breaths matching at last. After a little while, he rolled off, gathering her close to hold her. Little by little, she felt his breathing shift. Slow. And soon she realized he was asleep.

She lifted her head to make sure of it and found his eyes closed, his handsome face relaxed. Younger somehow, like his troubles had eased in his dreams. After all they'd been through, all they'd done, all he had yet to face, of course he was exhausted. She settled her head back against his chest and rested her hand on his flat stomach.

"Ripley," she said softly, then shook her head. "*Cam.* I love you, too. I love you."

He didn't stir, which was by design, of course. She could only confess the truth of her heart when she knew he wouldn't be able to respond. When she wouldn't stir whatever hopes he had that could only cause him heartache in the end.

But she *had* to say that she loved him. And she had to hope she loved him enough to save him in the end. Even from herself.

CHAPTER 17

The next morning, Ripley sat in the parlor of a home he'd ridden by over the years, casting side glances at its fine pillars and white stone facade, wondering who stood behind its windows, but never stopped at. His father's home. Or one of them. The Earl of Pottinger had several, of course. His grandfather, the duke, even more.

And all while Ripley's mother had lived in her little house, mourning the loss of a love that had been so cruelly snatched from her. Eventually dying with Pottinger's name on her lips.

The hatred Ripley felt was like a fire in his chest and it was only Jane's gentle hand in his that controlled it. She smoothed a thumb along the top of his hand.

"I'm fine," he lied. She didn't respond but arched a challenging brow. He smiled despite himself and lifted her hand to his lips. "I'm...*tolerable*," he corrected.

"And I'm sorry," she said, and not for the first time. She'd been saying it every so often all morning. They both knew why. It was only because of Nora that he was here, and Jane took responsibility for that and the pain that came with it. A foolish thing since he would endure a great deal more pain than this to help her. He'd burn alive to do that.

The door to the parlor opened and Jane withdrew her hand as the stern butler who had met them earlier stepped in and announced, "The Earl of Pottinger."

They both rose and watched as a tall man entered the room. Ripley had seen the man before, of course, in passing, but it was always a shock to see one's own features on visage of a stranger, even as an older version. Ripley had his mother's eyes, but the shape of him was this man. Though certainly the earl was more a tamed dragon than a wild one.

The butler stepped out, closing the door behind himself, and the earl took a little breath before he crossed toward Ripley with a hand outstretched. "Mr—Mr. Ripley. I'm so pleased to finally make your acquaintance."

Ripley blinked but didn't take the outstretched hand. He wasn't certain how he expected his father to greet him, what would have made him calmer rather than angrier, but this wasn't it. Pottinger spoke to him like he was some stranger. Or worse yet, just the famous former fighter that men of his ilk liked to trip over themselves to meet, even though they considered him beneath him.

"My lord," he said softly, and instead of shaking the hand still outstretched, he touched Jane's lower back. "This is my—my—Miss Kendall."

His father's gaze slid to her and his brow wrinkled, like he vaguely recognized her. Of course he would. He'd likely seen her in places like the Donville Masquerade. Once again, Ripley's anger flared. His father had continued with his mistresses and courtesans and lightskirts even though all the while Ripley's mother had withered and died.

He clenched his teeth. He was here for Jane, not to have a long-denied showdown with his father. He would *not* jeopardize her ability to find out where her sister was.

"Miss Kendall." The earl inclined his head and then glanced at

Ripley and back to her. "Welcome to my home. Please, won't you both sit? It will be more comfortable."

He and Jane returned to the settee, the earl took the chair across from them. For a moment there was only silence until his father filled it. "I-I've heard your club does very well. All my friends and their sons are members. I always recommend it to people, and did so especially at the beginning when you first opened it."

Ripley glared at him. Was this man taking some kind of credit for his success? Acting as though men came to his club because an earl had suggested it, rather than because Ripley had been a cham-pion? A fighter because he'd had no choice?

"Am I supposed to thank you?" he snapped, that anger bubbling up to the surface.

Jane reached for him, took his hand again without looking at him. She settled it against her knee, covered it with both her own, like she was offering shelter to some small part of him. To his surprise, he *felt* sheltered by her touch.

"No," the earl said swiftly. "N-No, of course not. I only meant that I've been aware of your success. Proud of it."

Ripley pressed his lips together, swallowed back every retort that bubbled in his mind, every anger he'd ever felt toward this self-ish, entitled man. He was here for Jane. He had to focus for Jane.

"If we've done enough of the pleasantries, perhaps we could move on to why Jane and I are here."

The earl nodded. "Yes, of course. May I call for tea or some other refreshment?"

"No," Ripley said. "Where is your son, my lord? One of your legitimate sons? He goes by Hugo."

Pottinger's nostrils flared slightly. "What do you know of Hugo? Why would you be seeking him?"

Ripley drew a shaky breath, but before he could say anything, Jane leaned forward. "I have a younger sister, my lord. She has apparently met your son, there was an attachment of some kind which developed between them and she…she's missing now. There's reason to believe he may know where she is."

Pottinger's jaw tightened. Once again, Ripley realized with a start how much he looked like the man. How he hated that. "What is your sister's name, Miss Kendall?"

"Honora Winchester, sir," she said. When the earl arched a brow, Jane added, "We have different fathers. She also goes by Nora."

"*Nora,*" the earl repeated, but it wasn't said in a neutral tone. No, he sounded frustrated. Exhausted.

Ripley leaned forward. "You know that name?"

His father glanced at Jane again and then refocused on him. "I…I had become aware that Hugo had met one of the young women who attends the seminary not far from our country estate. He seemed smitten, was asking me for permission to formally court her. I said no, of course."

"Of course?" Jane asked softly, but Ripley felt her tense at the instant dismissal of her sister.

He glanced at her again apologetically. "We are a family of title and wealth, Miss Kendall. And I…I looked into your sister's background. Although I was unaware of your attachment to Ripley, I did find out about your mother's past…and your own. You're a woman of the world, you must understand why a connection between my family…my legitimate family…and yours would be untenable."

Jane turned her face slightly and her tone became brittle. "Certainly."

"Do not turn your face away from him as if you're less," Ripley said, squeezing her fingers gently. "Never do that, Jane. He doesn't deserve that deference."

"Ripley," she whispered. "You don't have to—"

"You knew about this relationship he had or desired to have with Nora," Ripley snapped as he turned his attention back to Pottinger. "So you must know that if she disappeared, it is likely with him. I ask again, where is he?"

"See here," his father said, almost gently. "You're very angry, that's apparent. I cannot just send you after Hugo to mete out some justice. Not only do I think he would be defenseless against you, but there are appearances to be maintained. Protected."

"Protected," Ripley repeated, all the pains he'd felt as a lonely child making new appearances. Stealing some of the control he'd so carefully crafted to protect himself from them. "You *dare* to speak to me about protection? To tell me you wish to protect your son when you knew about me? You must have known about my mother's situation. And you did *nothing*."

He hated that there was a quiver to his voice and he snapped his mouth shut. He didn't want to show that vulnerability to this man. And he also knew he was dancing precariously close to the edge where the earl might simply deny Jane any further information about Hugo's whereabouts. They could possibly still track him, but without Pottinger's help it would take far longer. Ripley had to set his own feelings aside for her. He would not fail her as so many selfish men in her life had done before.

The earl shifted and at least had the decency to look slightly chagrined. "I know I wasn't present for you, but look how strong it made you. It made you a champion, a *fighter*."

Jane made a soft sound in her throat and to Ripley's shock she staggered to her feet. She stared at his father, a man with fifty times her power, and held him in place with the strength of her rage.

"You judge that as a good thing? The pain people like us suffered, it didn't make us stronger. It made us *broken*. You cannot break a person and then claim credit for how they survived, as if you did them a favor." She motioned toward Ripley with a trembling hand. "Campbell Ripley is powerful and good and decent *despite* you, my lord. Not because you abandoned him and his mother."

Ripley couldn't take his eyes off her. All this time he'd fought to protect her, as was his nature. But now she stood, sword unsheathed, eyes flashing, ready to go to war without thought to the cost.

His father opened and shut his mouth, his eyes wide. Ripley

wasn't certain if that was because he was shocked that someone like Jane would speak to him this way, or truly taking in her words.

Then he bent his head. "I-I failed you, Campbell. I failed your mother. And I'm sorry."

Ripley caught his breath. *There* was the apology he'd never thought he'd receive. The one he'd dreamed of as a boy when he stared at the cracked ceiling, when he listened to his mother softly cry in another room. Or watched her pack up to go live with a lover, her eyes hollow and sad as she left him with a friend or a neighbor because her current protector didn't want another man's by-blow around in whatever accommodation he provided her.

He shook his head. "If you are sorry, *truly* sorry, then you will do as I ask and tell me where Hugo is. Jane is the most important person in the world to me, the only one who has any real meaning in my life. I want to help her find her sister."

"If he truly loves her, if he has defied your edict to walk away, then there's no threat to him from us," Jane said.

"Yes. That would make him a far greater man than his father. *Our* father," Ripley said.

"And if he hasn't? If he has only kept her? What then?" Pottinger asked. "You still ask me to trade away the security of one son to the other."

Ripley sighed and looked at Jane. She nodded, as if she understood. "If he is as craven a coward as our father has turned out to be," he said slowly, and turned his gaze back on the earl. "Then Jane and I will simply remove Nora from his company. There will be no consequence, at least none to him. Just as your kind like and expect it, entitled as you are."

The earl let out a shaky breath, shifted on the settee. It seemed he was having a struggle and so both Jane and Ripley remained silent to allow that to continue. If it led to what they desired, Ripley could wait.

At last, the earl shook his head and said, "Hugo is my youngest son. When he came into his majority, he was gifted an estate just outside of London. It's rather run down—he rarely goes there—but if I were to guess where he might take someone, where he might escape, that would be it."

Jane sagged next to Ripley and he wrapped an arm around her, no longer giving a damn what his father would think of it. He locked eyes with the man. "Thank you, my lord. And now we'll trouble you no longer."

As he stood, so did the earl. Pottinger was very pale now, eyes wide. "I-I loved your mother." That stopped Ripley in his tracks. "And when you say I'm a coward, that's true. I didn't defy my own father to be with her, much as I desired to do so."

Ripley pinched his lips together. Some good that so-called love did him or his mother now. But it could still do some good for Jane and for her sister, and even for Pottinger's youngest son. "If you are truly sorry for your actions, then if Hugo *has* eloped with Jane's sister you will show him more consideration than you were shown."

The earl seemed to ponder that and then he nodded slowly. "I-I cannot speak for his grandfather. The duke won't be happy with this turn of events if it has gone that way. But I'm not powerless. I won't deny Hugo and any woman he marries the same future and support that I would give his older brothers. I...I promise you that, Ripley."

"Good," Ripley said. "Then we'll leave you."

If the earl wished to stop them, wished to make some further connection with Ripley, he didn't make a move to do so. He let them go with only a soft *goodbye*.

Jane held tightly to Ripley as they returned to the drive and the phaeton the earl's man brought around for them. After they'd entered the vehicle and Ripley urged the horses to ride, she looked at him.

"Ripley," she said softly.

He shook his head. "Not—not yet, Jane. I cannot think about it or talk about it yet. Let's focus on your sister, finding her and deciding our next step."

She reached a hand up to tangle through his hair as he drove. It was a loving action, a soothing action. "Whatever you want. Whatever you need."

And as they drove in silence for a while, he knew that what he needed more than anything was her. In his life, at his side, fighting his demons just as she'd done a few moments before. When this was over, he hoped she'd still be there to do just that.

CHAPTER 18

Jane and Ripley had been driving at a fast clip in his phaeton for hours, heading ever closer to the estate where she prayed she'd find her sister. But as much as she thought of Nora as they made their way, she also couldn't help but watch Ripley. He was so quiet, so withdrawn, that it had begun to frighten her.

His encounter with his father had been devastating. She'd heard that in every small waver of his voice, felt it in the shifts of him, seen it in the flickers of heartbreak in his eyes. She'd been powerless to do anything about it.

"He…he said he loved my mother," Ripley said, out of nowhere. "Pottinger."

She blinked and turned toward him, resting a hand on his thigh. The thick muscle there was tense. "He did."

"I know you read people, just as I do. It's in the nature of those in our position in life. But I can't see right now. I'm blinded by…by…"

"By what you went through," she supplied gently. "You can't look at this situation with detachment. No one would expect you could."

He swallowed and glanced at her briefly before returning his attention to the road. She recognized that not having to show all his vulnerability was likely the easier way for him to have this painful conversation. Even with her.

"Do you think that it's true? Did he love her?"

There was the tremble in his voice again, the edge of pain that broke her heart, made her picture this strong, powerful man as a small, helpless boy who wanted a father. Who wanted someone to come and save him and his beloved mother.

Jane considered the question, both through the lens of her own past and from what she'd observed. She thought of the way Pottinger had watched Ripley, how anxious he had been to connect with him, even if he'd done so entirely poorly. She thought of how the earl's voice had trembled when he said he loved Regina Ripley. How his eyes had changed.

"I think he did," she said at last. "Does it help to know it?"

Ripley sighed. "I don't know anymore. I want it to help. I want it to take some of the sting away. But is it better that he loved her and left? That he threw her away, threw *us* away, without a care even if she held his heart? Or is it better if he never loved her, if he used her up and discarded her like so many others did both before and after him? Those are my only two options and I'm not sure which is better and which is worse."

They were quiet a little longer. She stared off into the distance, toward the sun beginning to dip below the horizon. Ripley had called his father a coward, Pottinger had admitted that was true. And now Jane had to admit the same about herself. Ripley had offered her the exceptional gift of his heart. She was too afraid to take it, more willing to hurt them both by walking away than by staying and fighting at his side for whatever future they could build together.

If that wasn't a coward, she didn't know what was.

"Here is the estate," Ripley said.

She blinked and looked off into the distance. They'd just crested a hill and now there was an estate manor just coming into view, no more than a quarter mile away. It was a stone house with gabled windows and a porticoed entryway. Beautiful vines twisted up the stone and bright flowers bloomed along the green.

"If *that* is run down…" Ripley said with a low whistle.

She almost laughed, but before she could she realized three people were standing out on the circular drive, pointing up at the house as they spoke. Two were men she didn't recognize, but the third was a woman. Was it Nora? She hated that she didn't know because she hadn't seen her for so long.

But then the three turned as Ripley's phaeton reached them and Jane could see it *was* her sister. She recognized the dark blonde hair, the way she shifted her weight was just the same as she'd done when she was a little girl and nervous about something. And the fact that the young woman's hand slapped up to cover her mouth as if she were shocked when she saw them was reason enough.

Ripley had hardly stopped the high vehicle when Jane threw herself down, staggering a little as she rushed toward her sister. "Nora!" she called out. "Oh, Nora!"

She threw her arms around the young woman, unable to stop her tears as she held her, smoothed her hands across her shoulders, prove to herself that Nora was whole and unharmed. Nora patted her gently, but then withdrew, stepping back and out of her embrace.

Ripley had gotten down from the phaeton by then and came around. She felt him watching, felt him judging the situation and then his arm came around her to…to comfort her. She stared at Nora then, truly saw her, and realized her sister didn't look pleased to see her. She looked…irritated. Angry, even.

"Jane," Nora said, her voice unsteady. "What are you doing here?"

One of the men who had been examining the house had stepped away, but the other now joined Nora. Put his arm around her just as Ripley was doing with Jane. She realized this had to be Hugo. Of course it was. Just as Pottinger had, this young man had pieces that reminded her of Ripley. The hair, the way he held himself, his broad shoulders. A younger, easier version, like she could see what Ripley might have been if he hadn't been battered by a difficult life.

She preferred her version, even if she still wished she could take his pain away.

"Jane?" Hugo repeated, surprise in his tone. "Your sister?"

"Yes," Nora said.

He glanced at her and then over to Ripley. He caught his breath. "And you're...you're..."

"It seems none of us need introduction and yet that's exactly what we're going to do," Ripley said firmly. "I'm Campbell Ripley, this is Jane Kendall. And *you* are Nora Winchester—I see your sister in you."

"And I'm..." Hugo stepped forward, his gaze still locked on Ripley. "I'm Eldon Granger, but I go by Hugo. Your father...my father...your father..."

Jane gasped. "Then you know?" she asked. "You know Ripley is your brother?"

He nodded and then reached back for Nora. Their hands entangled. "Why don't you two come inside? We obviously have a great deal to discuss."

Nora looked at him, Jane noted the way he squeezed her hand. Offered support. And she knew. She knew that they were truly in love. That offered her solace, even if her sister's cold demeanor toward her didn't.

"Yes," Nora said softly. "Come inside."

They followed them in and were directed to a parlor just off the foyer. Hugo excused himself and Nora, apparently to arrange for refreshments, though Jane realized it was probably more to have a moment to digest this surprise arrival. Perhaps even formulate a plan of attack.

She used the time given for the same. She crossed to Ripley and he opened his arms, gathering her into his chest and pressing a kiss to the crown of her head.

"Now we know she's unharmed," he said. "Breathe, Jane."

"Yes. And if that's all I can have, I'll take it. But I still want to understand what the situation here is. And...and she hates me, Cam."

She lifted her face to look at him. His expression was so gentle and understanding. His touch as he stroked her cheek with a fingertip was soothing. "She's distant, yes. But I don't think she hates you, Jane. We'll work this out. I promise."

She smiled at him, even if she knew he couldn't truly promise that. But that he wanted to fix it for her meant the world to her.

The others returned to the room and Ripley released her. She stepped from his arms, her cheeks heating as she noted Nora's brief expression of disgust. Tea was brought in and Nora slipped away to prepare it. When she turned back, a cup in hand, she said, "I must correct something that was said earlier. You called me Nora Winchester, Mr. Ripley. I did go by that before, but now I'm...I'm Nora Granger. Hugo and I were married several weeks ago."

Jane had known it was likely true the moment she'd seen them pair off as a unit. She's seen the connection between them, felt it in a different way than one normally felt with a protector and a courtesan. Or even a man and his lover. Whatever there was there went deeper. But Jane still shut her eyes and let out her breath shakily at the news.

"You married," she whispered. "You ran away from school to marry."

Nora gripped the cup she still held a little tighter before she set it down with a clatter. "Do you mean that I escaped the prison you put me in? Yes."

Jane bent her head. She felt Ripley stir beside her, knew he wanted to say something to defend her, but she touched his hand and shook her head. "I-I think Nora and I might need a moment alone."

Nora folded her arms. "I don't want a moment alone."

"Please." Jane stood.

To her surprise, Hugo got to his feet, as well. He crossed to Nora and leaned in, whispering to her. It seemed he'd taken Jane's side in the argument, for at last Nora looked at Jane and then sighed. "Fine. A moment."

Jane glanced at Ripley, who had also risen. She shook her head. Now she was going to leave him with a half-brother he hadn't ever wanted to meet. "I'm sorry."

He shrugged and murmured, "The young man knows who I am to him. He and I probably need a talk as well. I'll feel him out for you, Janie."

She smiled up at him, this man she loved so deeply. Felt his love in return. Felt all he was willing to do and sacrifice just to keep her heart safe. "Thank you," she whispered.

Ripley strode toward his half-brother. "All right, Granger, tell me you have some stuffy billiard room and something strong to drink. I think we're going to need it."

Hugo was laughing, a little nervously, perhaps, as the men left the room and closed the door behind themselves. Which left Jane with Nora.

Her sister's arms were still folded and she remained across the room from her. "I almost wouldn't have recognized you," Jane said softly. "You've grown up to be so beautiful. So tall."

"You would have recognized me if you ever saw me over the years," Nora said, her tone clipped and cool. Then she sighed. "Honestly, Jane, why are you here? You made it clear you didn't give a damn about me when you sent me off to that school and abandoned me."

"I-I wrote to you." She swallowed. "Through others at first, but more after I learned to read and write."

"Oh yes. The letters. That will keep a girl warm during all those holidays alone," Nora said, and rolled her eyes.

Jane stared. Nora had done that as a little girl, too. She hated hearing how her actions had hurt her sister. But unlike their mother, who couldn't ever take responsibility for anything she'd done, Jane knew that she'd been wrong.

Even if she'd been trying to be right.

"I'm sorry," she said, and took a step toward her sister. Nora stiffened but didn't move away. That was enough for now. "I hate that you felt abandoned." She shook her head. "No. That's not right. I hate that I abandoned you. That I hurt you. It makes no difference, but I was trying to protect you and I had no understanding of how to do that properly."

"Protect me from the fact that you and our mother made money on your backs?" Nora asked. Jane flinched but didn't interrupt. "Do you know how I found out?"

"No." Her voice barely carried.

"When Hugo asked his father for permission to court me, the earl told him. My now-husband assumed I knew the truth from the start. He came to me to try to figure out together how to get around it. He told me. And it broke my heart."

Her sister's voice cracked and tears flooded her eyes. It all felt like a stab to Jane's heart. "I bungled this entirely. May I…may I try to explain now?"

"Do as you like, Jane. You have all this time." Nora turned her face, but Jane could see her watching from the corner of her eye. She was playing at being hard, but there was part of her sister that was curious. So Jane would give her the knowledge she desired and deserved.

"Yes, our mother is a lightskirt," she said.

"Still?" Nora burst out, her voice shaking.

Jane thought of their mother, worn and bitter in her depressing house. She had no doubts what she did to maintain the miserable life she was living. "Again. She married your father and was out of the trade for a while until…well, you know what happened. How he died. But she went back in after, I suppose because there's little choice for women like us." She thought of her shop. "Maybe at some point we just don't know anything else."

"And what about you?"

"I was a product of that world. A child from some unknown man. Not wanted, not planned."

Nora flinched. "Oh."

"Those eight years before you were born, she was…she's horrible, Nora. She dragged me through her life, never protected me from it. She would get drunk and blame me, even…even hurt me." Jane squeezed her eyes shut. "I hate telling you this. I wanted to protect you from this."

"But the secrets *didn't* protect me. Please have enough respect for now to tell me," Nora said softly. "I need to know."

Jane struggled for the words, which somehow felt so much more painful to say to her sister. But at last she found them.

"I thought it was over when she met your father. Winchester wasn't kind, but he steadied her. She focused on him, she was easier for those seven years. But when he died and she went back in, it all became so awful again. I felt like I didn't have any choice but to follow her. I had no other skills. I had to make money to try to help so she wouldn't…wouldn't…be worse."

"Oh, Jane," Nora's voice had softened even if she didn't move toward her. "But you were only fifteen."

"Some girls start even younger." Jane shrugged to dismiss it, even if she couldn't do that in her heart. Even if it was a wound that never fully healed. "I saw her starting to turn on you the way she turned on me. I was afraid she would hurt you, I was afraid she'd push you into the same life the two of us were leading. So I took you away and I put you in the school and I tried to keep you away from her. And from me. We would hurt you. *I* would hurt you. And I wanted you to have a chance at something better."

Now it was her voice that broke and she shook her head. Nora stepped toward her, holding out a handkerchief. "Here."

"No. I'm not going to cry. I don't want to manipulate you they way she always tried to manipulate me." Jane fisted her hands at her sides and forced her breath to calm and her tears to recede. "I didn't want you to go back to our mother's home during breaks and holidays. I certainly had nowhere to put you in London where what I was wouldn't be clear. Where my life wouldn't be an influence on you. And so I suppose I *did* abandon you. I thought that writing letters and sending gifts when I could would be enough. That you might not want more."

"But I did," Nora said. Her eyes welled with tears to match Jane's. "Sometimes a friend would bring me along on breaks, but mostly I sat in those empty rooms when everyone else was gone and told myself how you couldn't love me at all."

"I'm so sorry," Jane said. "It's not enough, not nearly enough, but it's true. I *never* wanted to hurt you, and I hate that I did."

Nora took a few breaths and she looked at Jane. *Really* looked at her, as she'd been avoiding doing since the arrival. She shook her head. "What you went through, it sounds terrible. And I…I do know how our mother can be. I started writing to her after I broke off contact with you. I found the address in some files."

"How did you do that?"

Nora shrugged. "Broke into the headmistress's study."

Jane closed her eyes, but she laughed a little as she shook her head. "I'm impressed and horrified in equal measure. Miss Knightly is terrifying—you were very brave."

"Thank you," her sister said with a little smile. "I wrote to Mother and she…she was dreadful."

"Yes, Miss Knightly gave me some of the things you left behind at the school. I saw Mama's letter telling you to land your Hugo so that you might have access to his wealth." She shook her head with renewed disgust at that. "Christ, at least she's predictable."

"That was the last straw," Nora said with a long sigh. "I'd hoped to find a connection, but it was obvious that wasn't going to happen. When she acted like I'd marry him to use him, I knew I had to protect him from her."

Jane smiled at the fierce way her sister lifted her chin. "You love him."

Now the pain fled Nora's face and she nodded swiftly. "Oh, how I love him, Jane. With all my heart. The idea that I'd ever take advantage of him was horrifying. I vowed never to speak to her again."

Relief filled Jane at that statement. "Good. I can handle her. Ripley is being kind enough to help me. Let me do that and protect you in some real way. A better way than I did before."

Nora looked her up and down. "It seems like Mr. Ripley protects you."

"Yes." Jane bent her head. "He does."

"Is that his formal title?"

Jane lifted her gaze. "Protector?" Nora nodded. "No. I left the trade a few months ago, thanks to the generosity of a friend who I helped through her own dramas. And Ripley is...Ripley is something else."

"You love him." Nora said. Not asked. Stated.

Jane ignored it. "What about this Hugo fellow? Your husband. Is he good to you?"

"Oh yes," Nora said with a wide smile that lit her up like a dozen candles. "He is wonderful, Jane. So wonderful."

"Good. You deserve wonderful." Jane sighed. "I won't ask for forgiveness for those years you were alone. But know that I do love you with all my heart. And all I want is for you to be happy."

Nora nodded. "Thank you."

Jane realized that was the best she would likely get for now. "Why don't we make sure the gentlemen aren't...having difficulty?"

"Yes."

They looked at each other for an awkward moment and then Nora motioned toward the door. "I'll lead the way."

Jane followed her, realizing with a start that her baby sister was now lady of this house. Married to the Honorable Eldon Granger, linked to an important family. She was out of Jane's sphere for good now.

And though she had hopes that it would lead to her happiness, there was still a sting of yet another person lost to her. Both because of what she'd done, and because of who she was.

CHAPTER 19

The first few moments after Hugo led Ripley into the billiard room were awkward at best. The young man was nervous, shifting around, nearly dropping the bottle before he poured them each a whisky and brought the glasses back.

He motioned toward the table. "Do you play?"

Ripley snorted. "No. That's a rich man's game."

Hugo bent his head. "My apologies. Why don't we sit by the fire? I'd wager we both have questions for each other after all these years."

Ripley wondered what questions this young man would have for him, but he followed him nonetheless and took a comfortable seat beside him. For a moment, they stared into the dancing flames together. Then Hugo turned toward him.

"How old are you?"

Ripley had just taken a drink and he almost choked at the unexpected question. He coughed and managed to regain control of himself. "Er, twenty-nine this past March."

Hugo let out a long sigh. "Fucking Father."

"Why do you ask?"

"Oh, it's just the same age as my eldest brother, Archibald." Hugo shook his head. "That means he was with your mother and our mother at the same time. Just as we always suspected."

Ripley pinched his lips, once again hating the earl for the harm he'd rained down on his mother. "When did you find out about me? About her?"

"Archie was about fifteen," Hugo said. "Lewis was twelve, I was eight. We overheard him talking to the Dreadful Duke. My apologies, that's what we all secretly call our grandfather. They were arguing about something…the subject turned to you. Father wanted to provide some schooling for you, some support, and my grandfather was railing at him about it."

Ripley shifted. So the earl *had* made some half-arsed attempt to provide. Again, he wasn't certain if that made the situation better or worse. "You three must have hated me."

Hugo blinked and looked truly confused. "Hated? No. Angry with him, certainly. Our mother wanted him to love her so desperately."

Bitterness filled Ripley's mouth. "It seems to be a habit of the women he bounced along on a string."

"Your mother, too?" Hugo said.

They stared at each other for a moment, understanding blooming between them. And while Ripley was still wary of this man, he also felt the tenuous beginnings of a connection.

"Well, when you started boxing, the three of us got *very* interested. I think Archie even attended a couple of your fights before our grandfather found out and banned him from doing it again. But we would read about them in the papers. I recall all three of us huddled around the paper, reading out the descriptions of your fights with bated breath. I wanted to crow to my friends when you won your first championship, but I knew Father would be livid if I revealed the relationship."

"You…you were *happy* to know about my life?" Ripley said.

Hugo nodded. "Yes. All three of us. When you started the boxing club and everyone in our acquaintance was joining, all three of us longed to do the same. Father said no once again."

"Well, bollocks to him," Ripley said with a shake of his head. "If you want to learn, you're welcome, all three of you. Membership fees waived. We don't have to acknowledge our shared blood."

Hugo blinked. "You'd do that?"

"It's not your fault, is it? What happened." Ripley shrugged. He acted like it didn't matter. Like he didn't want to see his other two brothers. To know all three of them a little.

"I'll tell them," Hugo said softly.

"But now I must ask you a more pointed question, don't I?" Ripley said. "You know what I must ask."

"You want to know about me and Nora," Hugo said. "You want to make sure that she's taken care of so that Miss Kendall isn't hurt."

Ripley nodded, spearing him with a long stare. Hugo straightened beneath it and cleared his throat. "I love her. I've loved her since the first moment I saw her through the fence of that school. Honora is everything I've ever wanted in my life, and I will love and protect her for the rest of my days."

There was an honesty there. A truth to those words. And even though Ripley didn't entirely trust that a man like this, raised with every advantage and privilege, would retain that powerful emotion he felt now, at least in the moment he meant it. Since they were married, that was good enough.

"I even defied Father for her," Hugo added with a sigh. "I know there will be consequences, but we'll face them together."

"I think you may find him easier now," Ripley said.

Hugo's eyes went wide. "What?"

"How do you think I found you?" Ripley said with a little smile as he sipped his whisky at last. "In exchange for my promising not to tear you apart limb by limb, he said he'd support you in your choices if it turned out you had married Nora."

"Was—was tearing me apart an option?" Hugo asked with a little gulp.

Ripley chuckled. "I suppose it would have depended upon the condition we found Nora in."

Hugo smiled, but it was weak and slightly terrified. Good. That was what Ripley intended. If he someday decided to betray Nora, at least he'd think twice about the consequences.

There was a light knock on the door and then it opened. Nora stepped in first, smiling at Hugo as both men came to their feet. Jane was behind her and Ripley frowned. She appeared drained, as if the weight of everything she'd gone through had finally come to bear.

"May we join you?" Nora asked.

Hugo held out a hand. "Of course, love." As Jane stepped up next to Ripley, he smiled at them. "Why don't you join us for supper and then spend the night here?"

Jane glanced at her sister. "Oh, that's so kind, but we've descended upon you uninvited to begin with and I wouldn't want to impose on you any further."

"It's far too late to return to London, Jane," Nora said softly. "It's no imposition. Please. I'll have Colepepper get rooms ready for you and add two places to the table for supper."

She gave a little bow of her head and then slipped away. Hugo smiled at Jane. "Would you like a drink, Miss Kendall?"

She nodded. When Hugo had stepped away, Ripley stared down into her face. "Did it go well?"

She shrugged rather than answered and when Hugo handed over her drink, she took half of it in a gulp. Ripley wanted to comfort her, but Nora returned then. Her smile was tight, but not as filled with tension and anger as it had been before she and Jane talked.

"It's all being arranged," Nora said. "Supper will be ready in half an hour. Until then, would you two like the tour of our home?"

"It's falling apart, but we're working on it," Hugo said with a laugh.

"Yes, of course," Jane said. "I'd love to see it."

Hugo and Nora linked arms and guided them out. Ripley took Jane's arm, as well, but as they were led from room to room, he could see, and more to the point, he could feel that she was just holding on. So all he could do was pour his strength into her and hope that it would be enough.

After the tense conversation between her and her sister, Jane was happily surprised that the supper was less so. As much as she doubted Granger, he was difficult not to like. He was friendly and amusing, and he clearly wanted to impress the two of them. Ripley because it was evident he was fascinated by his half-brother, and her because he wanted to make things easier for Nora.

Perhaps because of that, Nora also seemed happier. She was animated when she spoke of the house and their plans. She would fit into the world she had married into. It would be difficult, of course, but she was more of that world than Jane's.

Besides, Jane had every intention of using her connection to her friends like Esme, Marianne and Clarissa to ensure Nora was welcomed at least by a few ladies of quality.

Now they were finishing up their main course of the supper, a fine lamb shank with roasted vegetables, and Jane finally asked the question she'd been dying to know. "How did you two meet then?"

Nora stiffened a little, as if she anticipated this was a way for Jane to oppose the match, but Granger had none of the same reaction. His face lit up and he reached to Nora's hand where she sat at his right and squeezed.

"I was riding my horse past the school when he threw a shoe," he explained. "So I climbed down, and I admit I was swearing a rather blue streak out of frustration, trying to get him situated when I heard this musical laughter coming from behind the fence."

Nora relaxed a little and laughed that very musical laughter even then. "He was just so funny because he was apologizing to the horse for his language even as he swore, telling him he wasn't to blame for any of it."

"Well, to be fair, dear Vincent had done nothing wrong."

"Your horse's name is Vincent?" Ripley asked with a chuckle.

Hugo nodded. "I like human names on animals. My childhood dogs were Adam, Stephen and Bernard."

"Oh, we should get a dog, Hugo!" Nora said. "I've always wanted a dog."

Hugo looked at her with nothing less than utterly pleased indulgence. "Then a dog you shall have, my love. And you'll name him or her." He brought his attention back to Jane and Ripley. "Anyway, I looked up to see who was laughing at my situation and there was this angel, all haloed in sunlight. I was helplessly smitten."

"From then on we would meet at the fence and talk," Nora said. "I looked forward to those meetings all the time. I couldn't wait to see him."

Jane glanced at Ripley and found he was looking at her. She'd had the same experience with him, though her meetings were at far more unsavory places than a fence at a seminary for girls. But seeing him at the Donville Masquerade or at fights…those had been the highlight of her life for years. The thing that dragged her through the worst moments. She'd always taken a deep breath and reminded herself that at least she would see Ripley again.

"What about you two?" Hugo asked.

Ripley shifted as if he felt the discordance between the sweetness of Nora and Hugo's story and the harder edges of his own with Jane.

"She came to a fight," he said at last. "I saw her in the crowd and couldn't take my eyes off her. I haven't since."

"Ah, love at first sight." Hugo tipped a glass toward him with a wide, sweet smile. "Isn't it grand?"

Ripley looked at her and beneath the table he covered her knee gently. "Yes. It is."

Her cheeks heated as she looked at her plate. There he was, easily sharing the fact that he loved her. He never even hesitated even though she hadn't given him any of that in return. Just like she had done with Nora, it seemed all she could do was hurt him by trying to protect him.

She cleared her throat as the empty plates were taken. What she wanted was to run away from all this. From the good and the bad, the guilt and the joy. But perhaps she'd been doing just that for too long. So she smiled and nodded as her sister suggested that they have drinks after supper, play cards together. Like this was just... normal.

Could this be normal?

She shook away the thought and watched as Hugo took Nora's arm, the way she looked up at him with such love. And she saw the same expression on Ripley's face as he reached for her.

"How did it go with her?" he asked softly.

She blinked, trying to quell the sting of tears. "Complicated. I caused her a great deal of harm in my attempt to keep her safe."

He stiffened. "She must see why you did as you did."

"I think she does on some level. Her exchanges with my mother made it clear what she was, what she is. But...but that doesn't change that I abandoned her. That she was alone. Still, I think we have a chance to rebuild. Though perhaps it would be better if I stay away so I don't taint her life as a gentleman's wife."

Ripley stopped in the hallway, ignoring that Hugo and Nora had disappeared into a parlor. He cupped Jane's cheeks and tilted her face toward his gently. "She would be lucky to have you in her life."

When she looked into his face, she could almost see herself through his eyes. Could almost believe him. She smiled.

"Do you know any card games that a gentleman might play with his lady wife?"

"None that aren't slightly filthy," Ripley said with a chuckle.

"Well, then I suppose they'll teach us the rules," she said, and turned her face into his hand to kiss one of his palms. "Let's join them."

And so they did, and indeed her sister and Ripley's brother taught them to play. It was a good night, one she knew she'd treasure for a long time to come.

But it didn't change that now she had to decide what her own future looked like. And if she was brave enough to fit Ripley into it.

CHAPTER 20

Ripley could help but find amusing the fact that when Nora had arranged for the rooms for them for the night, she had given him and Jane separate chambers. Something a lady would do.

Despite that large difference, Nora was very much like her sister in a great many ways. Their laugh was the same. When they laughed together, he was fascinated by that fact. And her eyes were similar, that blue that felt like the depths of the sea. They tilted their heads the same way when they listened, Nora even fluttered her hands when she talked, which Jane occasionally did when she was truly excited by a subject.

But when it came to their lives, they were almost different creatures entirely. Jane was jaded. Of course she would be after the life she'd led. He didn't view that as a negative, of course. He, himself was jaded. It was a way the two of them matched.

Nora was innocent. Jane had succeeded in that by secreting her away at the school. And she had learned refinement there, too. She poured tea like a lady, she spoke like a lady, she acted like a lady. Even when she told the occasional story of rebellion during her years at the seminary for girls, they were gentle insurrections.

Taking extra sugar for her tea, sneaking into the headmistress's office.

And so now Ripley lay on a bed in a finely appointed chamber aside from a little peeling wallpaper here and there, staring at a carved ceiling…alone. He had no idea what would happen next. Jane had found Nora. He could see they would ultimately repair the damage done by their separation. They would become closer and that would be good for Jane.

But his part in her search was over and he feared more than anything else that she would push him away for good. That she'd run from the feelings he'd shared with her before, as was her nature.

There was a soft knock at his door and he glanced at it. He knew instantly that it was Jane there, like a tracker on a scent. He just knew.

Slowly, he got up, trying to slow his racing heart and opened the door. Her blonde hair was down around her shoulders, she had a dressing gown that had to be her sister's tied tightly around her. She looked up at him, her face soft in the dim light of the hallway lamps.

Wordlessly, she reached for him and he drew her into the room as she kissed him. There was no desperation to her kiss, but there was yearning. Need, and not just of the physical kind. So he gave, drawing her to the bed, untying her robe and finding her gloriously naked beneath.

He drew back to look at her in the soft firelight, memorized all the wonderful curves of her, just as he was always doing any time he was with her like this. He was clad only in his trousers and she touched his chest, sucking in a breath as she traced the lines of his muscles, the little tracks of scars from fights both in the ring and in life. Her fingers sparked pleasure, as did her lips when she pressed them to his throat.

He bent his head back with a little moan and drew his fingers into her hair, combing through the silky length of it as she tasted and teased him. She drew her mouth lower, over his chest, down to his stomach. She was unfastening his fall front as she did so and lowered it slowly. His cock brushed her stomach and he gasped with the ricochet of pleasure the contact created.

She smiled up at him and then she dropped to her knees before him. He might have protested, but she caught him in hand before he could and all words emptied from his sensation-addled mind. She stroked him and then she licked him, swirling her tongue around the head.

"Fuck," he groaned, low and long.

It seemed to urge her on for she took him deep in one long stroke, until he hit her throat, and then withdrew. The wet heat of her, the glide of her tongue, the suction she balanced so perfectly, it was all heaven and he surrendered. He supported himself with one hand on the high edge of the bed behind himself and held her in place with the other. She worked him with all her experience, taking him over and over, edging him toward release and then backing off to drag out the connection longer.

The pleasure was unreal, building up to a peak he wasn't certain he'd ever experienced before. She burned through his veins, every nerve ending was triggered and alive with her touch. He fought for purchase, but it was becoming a losing battle with every sweet sweep of her talented tongue. At some point he would lose control and while he wanted that, he also wanted more. He wanted her. He wanted mutual pleasure, he wanted to feel her ripple around him as she gasped out his name, his given name, in the flickering light.

He caught her elbows and she looked up at him, eyes wide. When he tugged, she didn't resist, but dragged her mouth back up the same path she'd followed down until their lips met. He reversed their positions swiftly, putting her against the edge of the mattress, lifting her to perch there. She wrapped her legs around him instantly and their bodies fitted like they were meant to do so.

Perhaps they always had been.

He adjusted slightly, reached between them to spread her wider. She moaned against his lips as he slid home into her tight body. And home it was, for *she* was home. She always would be, even if she convinced herself otherwise and walked away.

He shook that thought aside. Not tonight. Not now. That was a war to be fought later. For now he wanted this connection. He drove into her, loving how she lifted to meet him. Their short breaths mingled between kisses, their eyes held as they collided and withdrew. It was animal, but also gentle, it was heated, but also loving. They were tangled together, not just in passion, but in tenderness.

He never wanted it to end, but he only had so much control. When her pace quickened, when pleasure made her body grip and ripple around his, the sensation was too much for any man to bear. He gritted his teeth so he could ride out her release, draw it out until she was weak and panting with its power. Only then did he withdraw and let himself free. She stroked him until he came in a powerful burst of pleasure.

He collapsed forward, half on the bed, her legs locked around his waist. He kissed her neck, the spot behind her ear, she smoothed her hands along his spine and it was like everything in that moment was perfect. A space frozen in time, separate from whatever would come next.

And it was in that perfect moment that she let out a shaky sigh and said, "I'm a mess."

$\sim$

Ripley lifted his head when she said those words. "No, you are beautiful and perfect and lovely."

She smiled at how easily he said it. "No, I don't mean how I look. I mean...*I'm* a mess, Cam."

His brow wrinkled, but she could see he understood. Of course he would. They were the same in so many ways. They'd walked through fire and they both knew that it was a fairytale that someone could do that and not be burned. Permanently scarred. She didn't want to scar him even more.

"Love, everyone is a mess," he said with an almost indulgent smile.

She shifted from beneath him and scooted up to the pillows. She bent her knees and held them as she stared at him. He moved to lay on his side, watching her without trying to touch or distract her.

It seemed the time had come to say all the things they'd been waiting on.

"I've hurt the people I care about," she explained further.

"Of course you have," he said, and she flinched. He rushed to continue, "Because everyone does. It's a side effect of loving people, letting them in. It means we're vulnerable to being hurt and occasionally hurting them."

"But the last person I want to hurt is you, Cam. Because…" She drew a shaky breath. She couldn't avoid this anymore. Part of her didn't want to. "Because I do love you. And you scare me more than anyone I've ever known."

She could see him fighting his joy at her admission of her heart. See him trying to focus on her fears. "Why do I scare you?"

"Not because you're a fighter." She hesitated. "Well, perhaps because you're a fighter. Not just physically, but in other ways. You'll fight even when it hurts you." She reached up and touched the scar that slashed his eyebrow. "You are the kind of man who could fill up all those painful spots in me. It's so bewitching to think you could. And it's terrifying to think that I'd hurt you as a reward for that. That I'd take away from your life rather than add to it."

He nodded slowly. "But what if we healed each other?" he suggested, his tone gentle. "Because, my love, we've already done that for each other more than we've ever hurt each other."

She blinked. There was no denying he had helped her heal in these past few weeks. And before that, too. He had become the center for her, a place that was always soft when she fell there. A place that could bring light when it was dark.

"How have I healed you?" she asked.

"Do you think I would have gone to my father without you at my side?"

"Is that healing or tearing open a wound?"

He smiled. "Sometimes you need to do the second to get the first. I've hated him for so long, I've made him up to be this villain. But he was just a man. He's flawed, deeply flawed, and I'll never be close to him. But he doesn't loom as large in mind, and I doubt he ever will again. And my brother? Hugo? I think he was worth meeting. I'll meet the others, too. I'll come to know that part of myself because *you* gave me the strength to risk it."

She bent her head and moved on to her second mark against being together. "People will know what I was. Your father found out, others will do the same. Or untitled gentlemen will come into your club and recognize me as a lady who they passed time with in a hell. Will it bother you?"

"No. Not unless *they* bother you. And then they'll be very sorry they came into my club," he said. "Because my wife will not be bothered, not by anyone."

"Your wife," she repeated slowly, letting that word roll around in her mind. The most beautiful word she'd ever heard said by the voice she adored more than any other.

He nodded. "I never want to be without you, Jane. *My* Janie. I never want to wake up and not see you tucked into my side. I want to tangle up our lives so they'll never be separated. I want to share my name with you. I want to give you children—if you want them— that mix all the best parts of us. Children who will give us a chance to do better and give more than we were given. *That's* what I want. You and only you for the rest of my life."

Jane had known happiness in her life, very often at the side of the very man who said those words to her now. But until that moment, she'd never fully experienced joy. It was louder than anything else she'd ever experienced, it overwhelmed all else, all fear, all worst-case possibilities. It overtook everything but him. He shone at the center of it.

"Do you know why I learned to read?" she asked softly.

He seemed a little flummoxed that this was her response to what could only be called a proposal of marriage. But he, game as always, shook his head. "No. Why?"

"Because you wrote me letters and notes. Esme read them to me at first, but I…I wanted them to be *mine*. I wanted a part of you to be *mine*, Campbell Ripley. And now you're offering all of you. I couldn't refuse that. I won't. If you want to marry me, all I can say is yes. Forever yes to you, no matter what comes."

He did move on her then, almost with relief, like he'd wanted to touch her all this time and finally he could. His arms came around her, he drew her into his chest and their mouths met in what felt like the sweetest kiss of her life.

"Joy will come, Jane. Happiness will come. Good things will come. And we'll face the rest together."

"That sounds perfect," she said before she moved to cover him and celebrate this union, this surrender, the way she wanted to most.

L*ater*

They waited far longer to marry than Jane thought they would. Two months, to be exact, though for the entire time they lived together in his home above the boxing club, already bound by vows they'd spoken in each other's arms. Her fears, though not fully quelled, eased with every kiss, every promise kept by them both, every bright moment of joy.

So when her wedding day came and she stood in the center of the boxing club, which had been cleared and decorated for their friends to gather and celebrate them, it all felt right. Real. True.

Across the room she watched Ripley...*her husband*...as he talked with Brentwood and his wife Marina and all three of his brothers. The two months had brought much change for them. All were members of the club now, they came regularly to box. Eventually they'd started to come upstairs for supper together. Bit by bit, a tenuous relationship had developed between the four men. Warm and perhaps one day close. She'd seen how much that meant to Ripley, how it filled in some of what he'd longed for as a lonely boy and her heart swelled with happiness for him.

Nora was also there, though she stood with the countesses,

Esme, Marianne and Clarissa. She had been welcomed by them, of course, and it had eased her way a little in Society. Although, she didn't seem to mind when people outside their circle were cool to her. She loved her husband and she had her group of friends.

Somehow that group included Jane. Like Ripley and his brothers, the two of them had come to know each other over time. Grow closer. Find their way back to each other.

Esme smiled at her before she said something to the others and slowly crossed to her. She linked arms with her and together they looked out over the rest.

"Do you find your life here less boring than the shop?" she asked.

Jane jerked her head toward her friend. Though they'd discussed it before she found Nora, Esme had never spoken of the shop since. She'd simply been joyful about Jane's future with Ripley.

"Helping Ripley with the club? Working with the women, helping them train for bouts like I used to do with you? That…that's right. I wake up every day thrilled to come downstairs and start my day."

Esme put an arm around her. "Good. That's all I ever wanted. You saved me, Jane. I wanted to do something for you. But what you really needed was him."

The him in question turned toward them. Ripley's gaze moved over her, sensually possessive and deeply loving in equal measure. A man who wanted her in every way. More importantly, who *saw* her in every way and loved each vision of her.

"Yes. I needed him," she admitted. She smiled as he started across the room toward her, eyes locked on her with the same intensity he'd once sized up opponents in the ring.

"And now he's yours," Esme said with a little nudge. "And I assume none of us will be seeing you two for a while because I'm thinking this little honeymoon trip is going to last a while."

"Are you talking about our honeymoon?" he asked as he reached them. "You're right, Es, I think it will last a lifetime."

Esme laughed and then turned away, heading back to her own husband and leaving them alone.

"Good day, wife," Ripley said, and then gave a little shiver. "Oh, I like that."

"Excellent," Jane said as she wound her arms around his neck and drew him in for a kiss. "I like it better as the truth than a little lie we tell people to allow us to sleep in the same chamber."

"Speaking of that chamber, is it too soon to kick our friends out and take you upstairs?"

"I think two wicked scoundrels like us can figure out a way," she said with a laugh before she kissed him again without any of the fears that had once gripped her. Only the joy of certainty in him and the love that bound them.

EXCERPT OF THE LADY ONCE KNOWN AS

ABOUT AN EARL BOOK 5 (JULY 8, 2025)

Viscount George Lockhart rarely wore a mask to the Donville Masquerade. Why bother? He was known as what he was, after all-a rake. That was the mask he wore publicly and it had been all his adult life.

And now it was over. He would ride to his father's country estate tomorrow, a few weeks after that he would be married. It would fulfill an obligation, but...well, the whole thing felt so terribly empty.

He sipped his drink, and settled into a brood that made the sparkling hell a little less interesting. Or perhaps it was just that he was so jaded that the sex and sin around him didn't mean much. It didn't fire his blood anymore, or at least not the same way.

Sadly, neither did his future bride. He sighed as he thought of her. Miss Westinghouse, and he did only ever think of her as Miss Westinghouse, was beautiful. No one could deny that. She had a friendly face, dark blonde hair and pretty green eyes. If asked, he would have easily described her as beautiful, for she was. And he felt nothing about it. There was no zing of desire when he caught a glimpse of her across a room or when she smiled at him. There was no soft connection like he saw with his cousin and her husband or any of his recently married and blissfully in love friends.

George hadn't ever expected such a thing, of course. If someone had asked him a year ago about love he would have scoffed at the idea. It was harder to do so when one was so utterly surrounded by it as he was now. Still, though, deep feelings hadn't been a criteria when it came to his choice in a spouse.

He hadn't *had* criteria really, because he hadn't thought much of it. Until one day a few months ago when his beloved mother had pulled him aside and told him a secret. One that broke his heart. One that drove him to do what she wanted most for him: marry. She'd already chosen the potential bride, the contracts had been signed within days and here he was now. About to make the biggest promise of his life.

"Fuck," he grunted and slugged back the rest of his drink.

"You look like you could use another, friend."

He glanced up at the voice that had interrupted his brood and found Marcus Rivers approaching with a drink in hand. The proprietor of the hell was quite possibly the most interesting person George had ever met. He had swagger and confidence and an edge that could cut like a knife. He held sway over this den of inequity without raising much more than an eyebrow most nights. And he, like every other person George knew, it seemed, was desperately in love with his wife: Annabelle.

"Rivers," he said as the other man sat at the table beside him and together they looked over the writhing crowd of passionate attendees. Couples kissing, touching, playing games that had more to do with sex than chance. There was laughter on the air and desire along with it.

"You don't look very happy for a man who is about to take a bride," Rivers said after a moment.

George snorted. "I'd say you were a mind reader, but I don't think I've kept my expression schooled well tonight."

"If it's not something you desire, then I'm sorry about it, Lockhart," Rivers said. "Truly. Your world doesn't always allow for deeper feeling or passion, I know."

"You'll be extra sorry, soon, I think, for I know I'm one of your best patrons and I won't be attending the masquerade much anymore. If at all." George shook his head. "It wouldn't be fair to her, would it?"

Marcus gave a slight smile. "Ah, I knew you were a good man under all that rakish charm. So you intend to be a faithful husband, do you?"

"I would like to be better than I was raised to be, I think," he said softly, thinking of his father's mistresses over the years and how the existence of them had hurt his mother. The earl had slowed down in his later years and the two of them seemed to have come to an accord, but it didn't erase the betrayals. The hurts. The humiliations.

"Then this is your last night? Your last hurrah, it seems," Rivers said.

"Indeed." George drank the second drink as quickly as he had the first. Already he felt the little tingle of his senses dulling. Just enough to take the edge off.

"Then I suggest you go enjoy it rather than sitting at my table looking like a man about to be led to the gallows," Rivers said. "There is pleasure aplenty to drown your sorrows in."

He got up and George joined him. Rivers clapped him on the arm and said goodnight before he slipped off into the crowd. George let out a great sigh and looked around, this time with more purpose. Rivers was right. He could brood anywhere. The reason he'd come here tonight was to drive out his troubles in the body of some willing lady. He had to go on the hunt for the last time.

He drew a breath and looked around the room. There were women galore to choose from. Unlike him, most of them were masked, but he knew there were all kinds here, from the highest duchess to the cyprians using the safety found in this place to establish their relationships and settle themselves. Some he recognized as women he had indulged with before, but none drew his eye, even if he'd enjoyed his time with them. It was intensely frustrating, to be here for his final meal before the execution and find himself not hungry.

At least until *she* walked through the crowd. A woman in a deeply cut red gown and plain black mask, dark hair bound up loosely, curls bobbing around her cheeks and shoulders in a tempting waterfall that made a man want to trace the same path with his lips. He leaned forward, almost not of his own volition, tracking her graceful movements. Did he know her? It felt like there was some connection there, something instantaneous and hot that made him think he might have bedded her before. But no. He searched his memory and couldn't find her there in the tangled, foggy collection of merging bodies and mouths.

It was just that she drew him to her. Like a siren. He stepped a little closer, ignoring anything and everything else in the room but her. *She* was not as focused. Her dark eyes drifted from one place to another and beneath the edge of her mask, he could see her cheeks were pink with high color. Arousal or shock? Perhaps both. There was a tremble to those full lips that gave him the impression. Perhaps it was her first night here, perhaps she'd never seen such shocking things as the debauched pleasures going on around her.

He knew only one thing: he was going to find out. And if she was an innocent to the Donville Masquerade, he was very happy to be her introduction to all it had to offer.

He moved toward her, drawing a hand over his clothing to smooth it. One step, another and he noted the moment she became aware of his approach. Her eyes met his. Stunning eyes. Brown, but they sparkled in the candle and lamplight of the hell, filled with life and emotion. Her lips parted as that same gaze drifted over him from head to toe and made his body react along the same line as her stare.

He hadn't had such a strong reaction to a woman in a very long time. It was as intoxicating at the liquor burning in his body.

"Good evening," he said as he reached her.

That pretty gaze flitted away, toward the door and escape for a moment before she pushed her shoulders back and swallowed hard. "Good evening," she said, but her voice barely carried and was rough.

He smiled in the hopes it would soothe her. "It's a little overwhelming your first time, I know."

She blinked and there was no mistaking her surprise at the statement. "How-how do you know it's my first time here?"

He leaned a little closer. "You have the look about you. A little like a rabbit trying to avoid a trap."

"And would that make you the hunter, sir?"

He shrugged. "Anyone can be a hunter in the Donville Masquerade…" He hesitated in the hopes she would provide a name. It wouldn't be her real one, but it would give him something to moan into her ear if this night ended as he hoped it would.

She worried her lip, forcing him to look at the fullness again. Wonder what it would taste like if he nipped it gently as she rose beneath him in pleasure. "I can't-it's-"

He cocked his head. "Not your real name."

"Oh. Yes." She let out a shaky sigh. "I suppose I do reveal myself as naive, don't I? My name…or at least my name here…is Aphrodite."

His brows lifted. "The Greek goddess of physical love?"

Her cheeks brightened further. "I didn't pick it."

He drew back at that statement. He'd thought this woman was a lady based on her hesitation, but now he wondered if she was a lightskirt. And perhaps not one here of her own volition if she hadn't even chosen her own secret name.

"If you're in trouble," he said softly. "You have those here who would help. I can bring you to Rivers. He and his wife would never let you be harmed."

She shook her head. "I-I don't know what you mean."

"You said you didn't choose your name, I thought you might have been forced to come here," he explained.

"That is a surprisingly protective reflex, sir," she said and her tone was now speculative, as if she had seen something in him she hadn't expected. "But no, I wasn't forced in any way. A friend encouraged me to attend, one who is far more experienced in the ways of the world than I. She chose my name, much to my chagrin once she told me what to use."

She smiled and he caught his breath. He could hardly focus at the brilliance of it as he nodded. "Good. I'm glad to hear it. I wonder, then, if you might dance with me."

She looked over her shoulder toward the dancefloor where couples were paired off, grinding together in ways that never would have been accepted in any ballroom in Society. Mouths merged, hands roved, it was all foreplay. In some cases, more than foreplay.

"Yes," she whispered, this time with a little more neediness to her tone. It called to him, beckoned to his own desire.

He held out a hand and she looked at it. It was ungloved, of course. The Donville Masquerade was a place for skin on skin. She looked at her own ungloved fingers for a moment and then took his hand. There was a shock of electricity that rippled up his arm when she did, a fascinating power that made his body tingle. At least he knew this last night would be explosive.

They moved to the dancefloor together and she shivered before she lifted her hand to his shoulder. He held her stare as they began to move, his hand dipping low on her hip, tracing the line of her there as his thumb stroked against silk.

She gasped at the contact and stumbled slightly, but he kept her upright as they turned in the milling crowd.

"What-what is your name?" she asked. "Or the name you give here."

So she didn't recognize him. Not a lady of his rank, then, or at least not one who moved regularly in his circles. He started at that thought, for he'd never been so interested in the origins of a lover at the masquerade before. Why was this woman different?

"If you are Aphrodite," he said softly. "Then let me be Ares."

She stared up at him. "Her lover?"

His nod was slow and meant to give his exact meaning. "If she would allow it."

Find The Lady Once Known As at retailers everywhere on July 8, 2025!

The Broken Duke

The Silent Duke

The Duke of Nothing

The Undercover Duke

The Duke of Hearts

The Duke Who Lied

The Duke of Desire

The Last Duke

To see a complete listing of Jess Michaels' titles, please visit:

http://www.authorjessmichaels.com/books

ABOUT THE AUTHOR

USA Today Bestselling author Jess Michaels likes geeky stuff, Cherry Vanilla Coke Zero, anything coconut, cheese and her dog, Elton. She is lucky enough to be married to her favorite person in the world and lives in Oregon settled between the ocean and the mountains.

When she's not trying out new flavors of Greek yogurt or rewatching Bob's Burgers over and over and over (she's a Tina), she writes historical romances with smoking hot characters and emotional stories. She has written for numerous publishers and is now fully indie.

Jess loves to hear from fans! So please feel free to contact her at Jess@AuthorJessMichaels.com.

Jess Michaels offers a free book to members of her newsletter, so sign up on her website:
http://www.AuthorJessMichaels.com/

facebook.com/JessMichaelsBks
instagram.com/JessMichaelsBks
bookbub.com/authors/jess-michaels